# Fever of the Colt

He came out of the desert, a tall grim man stooped in the saddle, on a horse as tired as he was. Deputy Clint Randall, for he it was, had just killed the murderous Tad Lester. He was only doing his duty and Lester had deserved to die but Clint had eyes only for Tad's sister Mary. But what chance did he have now, particularly as he suspected he'd have to put Mary's other brother, Rolf, into a long box if he didn't change his ways pretty quickly?

But the town of Laredo had major problems for gold bullion had been stolen from the railroad and whilst Sheriff Hoot Sampson was damn sure he knew the robbers, if not the mastermind behind it all, the suspects' alibis were rock solid.

Even so, Clint was determined to deliver hang-noose justice to the thieves and once he put his mind to something neither bullet nor cold steel would stand in his way!

# Fever of the Colt

GLENN MORTON

**A Black Horse Western**

ROBERT HALE · LONDON

© 1950, 2002 Norman Lazenby
First hardcover edition 2002
Originally published in paperback as
*Colt Fever* by Glenn Morton

ISBN 0 7090 7185 X

Robert Hale Limited
Clerkenwell House
Clerkenwell Green
London EC1R 0HT

Typeset by
Derek Doyle & Associates, Liverpool.
Printed and bound in Great Britain by
Antony Rowe Limited, Wiltshire

# 1

# IN-BITTEN
# RANNIGAN

He came up out of the arid desert, a tall, grim man stooped in the saddle, on a horse as tired as he was. His Stetson was yellow with desert dust. Where his red bandana hung round his neck, sweat had turned the dust into mud. On the left side of his flannel shirt was a tarnished star with the word DEPUTY on it. Behind him, on a rope, a led horse, flecked with dried lather, followed wearily.

Clint Randall licked dry lips, stared into the heat haze. He could see the distant town of Laredo, and the lawless town on the Texas-Mexico border was no mirage. He was back home after his three day, almost non-stop ride into the desert and butte country.

He settled back in the saddle, resting one arm on the horn. He was tired and worn out and grimly content to allow the passage of time to bring him into Laredo.

Without the rust stubble of beard, Clint Randall was a goodlooking, slow-smiling young fellow with a strong sense of justice which had prompted him to take on the job of deputy sheriff. With Laredo booming under the combined influence of cattle, gold and railroad construction, the job of a lawman was no easy one.

He was met three miles out of the town by a party of four men who were riding across the parched land with a thunder of hoofs. On sighting Clint Randall, they reined in at a wave from one of the men, and waited until the tired horse plodded down the trail.

'Howdy, Clint,' greeted the bulky man with the bristling red moustache. He jerked hard eyes at the weary, led horse. 'So yuh got him?'

'I got him, Sheriff,' assented Clint grimly. 'I got Tad Lester. He waited for me with a rifle, but I stalked round the galoot an' got him. He's buried now.'

'So yuh brought his horse back as proof,' returned Sheriff Hoot Sampson. 'Good fer yuh, Clint. Reckon thet'll show some o' the *hombres* in this durned town thet murder ain't no laughin' business – which is what too many o' 'em think it is! Reckon young Rolf Lester might quit ridin' herd with them gun-totin' rannigans who are makin' this town what it is.'

Clint nodded tiredly. He was thinking only one thought, and had ridden with it for hours. It was a grim, bitter nagging thought. *What would Mary Lester think of him when she learned he had killed her elder brother, Tad?*

Tad Lester, a red-blooded buckeroo with low-slung twin guns, had gone too far. He had shot up a railroad office at night. All might have been well had not a venturesome clerk grabbed at his mask. Then his identity had been revealed.

Tad had ridden out, presumably for the border. And Clint had gone out after him only minutes later, following the man's trail with the aid of a brilliant white moon. It had been a long ride into the desert country, with the trail-wise Tad trying all his tricks to shake off his lone pursuer. And the end had come in Colt-smoke after a day and two nights in the saddle.

'Wal, git yoreself some shut-eye, Clint,' advised Hoot Sampson, 'an' don't worry none. Reckon everythin' will work out fine in the end.'

He was trying to be kind in his rough fashion. Sheriff Hoot Sampson knew Clint had called on Mary Lester more than a few times, in spite of her two gun-happy, buckeroo brothers. Mary and her brothers ran the Circle Four ranch, raising Texas longhorns on the semi-arid range. Their father had died like Tad – in a gun-fight with the law. Mary, too, was a trifle wild – but fascinatingly pretty.

'Reckon we were on our way to the railroad,' said Sheriff Sampson. 'Bin another derailment an' a payroll stolen! Goldarn them owlhoots! Man can't rest more'n an hour in this durned town. Reckon I ought to git me another job where it's plumb peaceful an' quiet!'

The three other men, who evidently made a posse, guffawed derision. Then the four riders wheeled their big, sleek horses and thundered away across the cactus-covered valley.

Clint touched spur steel to his tired bay and the horse plodded on again. He himself sank low in the saddle. He was still thinking of Mary Lester. There was nothing else to think about. All other thoughts were as dry and harsh as the dust under his horse's hoofs.

He realised Mary would hate him.

He reached the streets of Laredo and came down the main stem to the sheriff's office. He took the two horses into the stable at the back of the big brick-built office and handed them over to the liveryman. He walked round to the front again, and, using his key, let himself into the building.

He passed Hoot Sampson's quarters. The sheriff was unmarried and lived here. Clint, too, had a room on the second floor. At the back was a big office and a passage which led to four iron-barred stone-built cells. The cells were empty right now. The men of Laredo seemed to prefer to die rather than be caught.

He washed and shaved, driving back the grim desire to lie down and sleep, then went to his room and changed, donning clean trousers of brown material, and a blue gaberdine shirt which stretched tight across his muscles. He got out a new fawn Stetson. He polished his boots slowly until the black leather was shining again, and wiped off the flecks of horse blood from his spurs. Feeling the desire to get rid of the desert completely, he donned leather, brass studded cuffs at his wrists and then pulled out some gloves from a drawer. His last act was to fasten leather riding chaps round his brown trousers.

He went out, on his way to the stable. He had told the man to have a fresh horse ready for him.

As he got to the boardwalk a brawny six-footer stepped forward and barred his way.

'Howdy, Rolf!' drawled Clint Randall.

The other's lips were a thin, tight line.

'Yuh killed Tad! I saw yuh ride in with his horse! By

God, I nearly plugged yuh, Randall. But I don't reckon to swing for a stinking, lousy lawman!'

Rolf Lester threw his gun-belt to the boardwalk with a sudden clatter. He'd had the belt half unfastened when he had barred Clint's path.

'Drop yore's!' hissed the big blond young buckeroo.

Clint smiled slowly, staring into the other's bitter eyes. He began to unbuckle his single belt with the two shiny holsters. He worked slowly, deliberately. He smiled at the other, and Rolf Lester's weatherbeaten face contorted with fury.

'Git thet damned belt off! I don't aim to git shot in the back. Why the slow play? Yuh figger the sheriff will be back? I kin tell yuh he's down at the railroad! Git yuh blamed hands up! I aim to beat yuh to pulp, Randall!'

Clint felt every tired muscle in his body slowly tense for a great effort. He had had no sleep for thirty-eight hours and little to eat. He had intended to ride over immediately to see Mary Lester. But first he had to fight her brother. He had killed one. Now he was being forced into fighting this young rannigan with the red-blooded strength of a Brahma bull.

Clint's belt dropped dully. Old in experience of rough-house, he stepped back. Rolf's fist which had slashed out wickedly as the gun-belt dropped, carved thin air.

Clint summoned his tired strength and rammed a fist to the other's solar plexus. The bones in his arm jarred. It was like crashing into rock. Then Rolf's left swung in a shuddering uppercut.

The gloved fist caught Clint before his slowed reaction could enable him to dodge. The terrific blow staggered him and he went backwards, falling from the boardwalk. In falling, he tripped and fell heavily in the dusty road. He lurched up and Rolf was immediately over him.

Clint scrambled up, threw a vicious left to Rolf's face using all his flagging energy. But Rolf Lester was still fresh and rode the punch with a short sneering laugh that breathed contempt. His arms forked out in fury but with the method of a piston. Savage blows jerked Clint's head upwards, clouding his senses and making him reel. His hands became incapable of quick reaction. His gloved fists tried to fend off Rolf's red-blooded pounding. He fell back against a post supporting the upper storey of the office. Rolf bored in and planted solid, relentless blows to Clint's face.

The deputy sheriff slid down the post, his mouth twisted as he sucked breath and gasped. He crouched on the dirt and then hauled himself up, using his two hands to grasp the post.

Rolf Lester was waiting. He watched Clint turn from the support of the post, and then he smashed his fists into the other man.

Clint swayed, eyes bleakly focussed on Rolf's head. His fists moved out slowly and Rolf slammed them down with a laugh. He planted a terrible right to Clint's chin and watched him fall with odd slowness to the earth.

Three or four hard-bitten rannigans had gathered to watch, but not one of them lifted a hand to help the deputy.

Rolf Lester shuffled closer to the fallen man. His blue eyes were bright with hate.

'Yuh won't be so quick with a hogleg when I'm

done!' he grated.

Clint's arm was outstretched as he sprawled, dazed. Rolf lifted his booted foot.

'I'll break every bone in yore right hand!' he said harshly. His foot was about to stamp down when a man who had pushed across the road walked through the small group of onlookers.

'Yuh kin keep thet foot up Lester!' he snapped.

Rolf Lester looked into a firmly held Colt. For a moment he hesitated, tempted to stamp on Clint's hand and to hell with the gun. Then, with his blue eyes flickering sardonic amusement, he stepped back, hooked his hands in his belt and surveyed the newcomer.

The man with the gun was Jesse Teed, a rancher of about forty years of age. He was a respected man in the town, and a friend of Clint Randall.

The deputy moved and rose laboriously while Rolf grinned into Jesse Teed's gun. Clint dusted his clothes, took deep breaths.

'Yuh shore messed me up, Rolf,' he said. 'Reckon I got to give yuh best this time.' He drew another deep breath and added quietly: 'But watch out, feller. Jest watch out!'

'Yuh kin watch out, too, Randall!' rapped back Rolf. He picked up his gun-belt then turned and strode across the road and went into a saloon. With graven faces, the handful of border characters who had watched the fight strolled off. It was just another brawl to them.

'If there was any damned law in this town, thet in-bitten Lester rannigan ought to be in jail for assault!' fumed Jesse Teed.

Clint smiled.

'Fergit it, Jesse. I reckon we kin call it a personal matter between me an' Rolf.'

The rancher changed the subject abruptly.

'Did yuh git his brother? Thet what he's so sore about?' Clint nodded.

'Yeah. I shot Tad while resistin' arrest. What else kin yuh do when a *hombre*'s layin' fer yuh with a Winchester?' Clint walked stiffly to the boardwalk. Jesse Teed watched him shrewdly.

'Yuh look all done in! Reckon yuh ought to git some rest, *hombre*. So that's why Rolf Lester beat yuh up! Reckon yuh could smash him if yuh were fitten!'

'Fergit thet as well, Jesse,' drawled Clint. 'I reckon I jest took a beating. Maybe I've had no sleep or rest fer thirty-eight hours, but thet don't mean nuthin', So long, Jesse. I'm still going to see Mary Lester at the Circle Four.'

He went into the sheriff's office to wash the blood from his face and knock dust from his clean clothes. Jesse Teed stood staring after him.

'Now there's a jigger who don't know when he's had enough.'

Some ten minutes later Clint Randall was riding a fresh horse down the well-used trail leading east out of Laredo. The Circle Four ranch lay well in Texas territory, and was about six miles out of town. Then the Circle Four range stretched into the rocky hills some twenty miles further on. In those hills, where steers often strayed in their search for grass, cholla cactus and Joshua trees flourished wherever there was moisture. And in the hot silence, rattlers basked on flat-topped rocks.

He knew he was terribly tired and acting the fool, but he wanted to see Mary; talk to her honestly before the story of his killing of Tad reached her ears in all the distortion that only rumour can provide. He just wanted to talk to her, that was all, and could not rest until he had done so.

But he still knew she would hate him.

With the wariness bred in him as a lawman, he left the trail as he approached the Circle Four ranch. He came through a rocky defile, where grass tufted in nooks and crannies, and then halted his horse to stare at the Circle Four ranch-house. The spread was not a big one or a rich one. Mary and Rolf employed only two other hands. Maybe they would have to hire another now that Tad, the elder brother, was dead.

The ranch-house was silent, with smoke rising from a chimney. Maybe Mary was cooking, for the day was too warm for a fire. He could see a few horses in a corral, and the pretty flower bed Mary Lester had made to brighten the front of the ranch-house. Of Mary, there was no sign.

He was about to jig his horse forward when he saw a buckboard rattle round the big cottonwoods and rush through the open gates of the ranch-yard.

Clint halted his horse and narrowed his eyes as he stared into the sun.

Mary Lester came to the ranch-house door, wiping her hands on her apron. Even the mere sight of her sent a strange longing through him. He wanted to ride up furiously and take her in his arms and tell her he loved her. But instead there was this watching; the wariness bred in him by encounters with lawless men.

Clint thought the man who drove the buckboard was Seth Mundy, one of the hands.

He was about to ride forward when he saw Mundy grab at the boxes on the buckboard. The man staggered into the ranch-house with the box, and swiftly returned for another. Clint waited, puzzled. He saw Seth Mundy unload four of the long, rectangular boxes and carry them into the ranch-house.

Clint Randall felt pretty grim. He did not like it. In his experience of western habits, long rectangular boxes of that description were used mainly for carrying bullion. The banks and mines used the long, narrow boxes for holding gold dust and chips.

He had seen Seth Mundy staggering under the weight of the boxes. What did they contain?

Maybe they were old boxes, bought at a sale and used to carry something heavy.

With sombre feelings, because deep down he had a hunch something was wrong, Clint Randall waited. He waited until the buckboard was unloaded and the horses unhitched. Then the buckboard was taken round to the barn. Only then did Clint ride out.

He came down slowly and rode into the ranch-yard. He hitched his horse's reins to a fence, and walked up to the front porch.

Even before he got that far, Mary Lester had seen him and she walked out.

Clint saw the fear in her blue eyes. He saw her smooth her cherry-red gingham dress. She had fine, spirited features with generous lips, but there was this fear on her face right now. Her honey-coloured hair fell in ruffled waves at the back.

'Mary, I want —' he began.

Seth Mundy came out of the bunkhouse. He had heard the clump of the horse's hoofs and the voice.

'Howdy, Deputy. Lookin' fer somethin', maybe?'

There was a curious note in the cowboy's voice. He was a lean waddy of indeterminate age. He badly needed a shave. His hands were black with dirt and his clothes were no better. Clint shot a glance at the unpromising specimen, wondering how Mary put up with it. He noted the man's hands were nowhere near his two guns. He did wonder why a cowboy should wear two guns.

'Jest hankerin' to talk to Miss Mary, feller,' drawled Clint.

Seth Mundy's eyelids fell as if he was searching for significance behind the innocuous answer. But he did not move away. 'Kin I talk to yuh, Mary – inside?' asked Clint quietly.

She nodded, as if lost for words.

'Tad didn't mean to kill! Where is he? He got away, didn't he?' she stammered.

He came up beside her on the porch. His hand fell lightly on her sleeve.She looked at him quickly.

'They are jest a bit wild – Tad and Rolf!' she said with an attempt at defiance. 'But yuh don't under-stand.'

'Mary – Tad didn't get away.'

She drew back and her blue eyes leaped to unnatural brightness.

'Yuh captured him?'

'I had to shoot him,' he said harshly. 'It was him or me.' She just stared back. Her cheeks went pale under her tan. She knew without asking that Tad was dead. It was in every grim line of the man opposite her.

'Look, Mary, yuh've got to understand!' said Clint urgently. 'I had to do it. I'm deputy sheriff. Tad killed a man. Maybe it was better fer him to go out shootin' than a – a – rope. Mary, I wanted to come here an' tell yuh about it myself afore the rumours git around. It was a fair fight. And, Mary, I want to help yuh.'

'Yuh want to help me!' she flashed. 'Yuh kill my brother and try to give me that fool's talk. There's nothin' yuh can say now, Clint Randall, that can make things all right between you an' me! Yuh need-n't come around here any more. Rolf was right – he said yuh were jest tryin' to get somethin' on Tad an' him. Get out, before I go for a shotgun!'

'Yuh heard, feller!' grated Seth Mundy, and his hands moved near his gunbelt.

'I wouldn't if I were yuh!' snapped Clint, and in a flash his hands were on his gun-butts.

He paused a moment undecidedly. Bitterly he saw the inevitable had happened between him and Mary Lester. Their friendship, which had survived the difficulties which Tad and Rolf had created, had crashed.

He walked down the porch steps and went over to his horse. At that moment the pounding of a horse's hoof-beats was heard, and a second later Rolf Lester rode furiously into the ranch-yard and dismounted.

When he came round from behind his horse he had a gun in his hand. It pointed at Clint.

'Maybe I ought to kill yuh now!' he snapped.

Mary ran down towards them. She came up, clutched Rolf's arm. She shook her head several times, and then found words.

'No, Rolf! No! Yuh fool, they'd hang yuh!'

'They'd have to prove it!'

'I said – no! Let him ride away!'

Something in Mary's voice caused Rolf to hesitate, and he glanced at her. Then he stared at Seth Mundy, and that fellow gave a queer nod of his head.

Ignoring everything, Clint jumped on his horse's back. He took up the reins and looked at Mary.

'Remember, Mary, when yuh want help, I'll be around to help yuh. An' yuh'll shore want it some-day!'

He rode out of the Circle Four ranch-yard with complete indifference to Rolf's gun.

He had seen the buckeroo was full of drink. The young fool had been in the saloon drowning his grievances in rye.

Out on the trail again, Clint just sank low in the saddle. It was not his usual riding habit. He was mostly a proud riding man and had a fancy style equal to any *hombre*.

But he felt suddenly overwhelmingly tired and despondent. Just as he had guessed, Mary hated him. The odds were all against their friendship turning into real love. For his part, he loved her. But she had been turned against him.

When he rode back to the sheriff's office, he found Hoot Sampson stamping around, glowering at the window and smoking furiously.

'Howdy, Clint. Still on the prod? Yuh know some-thin'?'

'What?'

'Thet wasn't a payroll thet was stolen from the

derailed car. It was bullion – twelve thousand dollars of gold in them long boxes!'

# 2

# GUNS AND GOLD!

Mary Lester was fighting back tears of bitterness. Suddenly she wheeled from the ranch window. She had watched Clint Randall ride over the crest of the trail and her heart was a whirl of confused emotions.

'Yuh fools – yuh awful fools!' she cried.

Rolf Lester looked back at her angrily. Seth Mundy stroked the leering smile on his dirty face with his equally dirty fingers.

'Yuh needn't worry none, Mary!' snapped Rolf. 'Thet bullion is a-goin' out o' here at sundown. No feller knows it's here.'

'Shore right, Miss Lester,' drawled Seth Mundy. 'Like the boss told me – I made a wide trail out by the salt lake. Shore figger no jigger saw me drivin' thet buckboard.'

'Your boss!' she said scornfully. 'I wish I knew the name of this boss! I'd shore tell him he can't use the Circle Four as a dumping-place for his robberies!'

'Reckon yuh'll have to play the bizness our way, Mary,' said Rolf harshly. 'Some men were killed in thet train robbery and —'

19

'Did yuh help to derail the train?' she flung at him.

'I've told yuh I was in Laredo.'

She rounded on Seth.

'But yuh were there! Yuh helped to kill men! There's too much killin' going on! Too much! Oh, what can I do?'

Rolf took out 'makings' for a cigarette and sent a grim glance to Seth. The bravado induced by the whiskey had now drained from him. He was just a grim, intent young western buckeroo.

'Yuh kin do nuthin', Mary, 'cept keep yore mouth shut. Like I said, the gold will go out at sundown. Yuh jest got to fergit about it till then. If the boss told Seth to keep it here, thet's the way it is.'

'The boss!' she breathed. 'I hate him! He's had yuh and Tad work for him - given yuh easy money. Yuh've neglected this ranch to go shootin' and heaven knows what else. An' now Tad's dead! Oh, I don't know what to think about anything!'

'Don't think. An' don't talk to that durned deputy. I tell yuh he's pizen to the likes o' us, Mary. He's jest a snakeroo. Reckon I've heard him boastin' in the saloons as how he'd git the Lester fellers by tawkin' to their sister. Wal, he's got Tad. Don't fergit thet, Mary. Don't yuh ever fergit he killed Tad!'

It was more than she could stand. She flung out of the living room and went into the kitchen. Blindly, she busied herself with her interrupted cooking. Her mind was a turmoil of confused thoughts. She just could not think straight, and the only outstanding facts were the ones Rolf had just hammered at her. Tad was dead, and Clint Randall was the man who had hunted him down!

There had been a time, a few weeks back, when life had been fairly placid for a week or two, when she had thought she was falling in love with steady Clint Randall. But Tad and Rolf had made her doubt him. And now everything had been whirled violently upside-down.

For an hour or so she worked furiously, trying to chase out of her mind the knowledge that four boxes of stolen gold were hidden in the ranch-house cellar, beneath her very feet!

The thought of it was sheer agony. Every few minutes she stopped in spite of herself to stare out of the window, expecting the drum of horses' hoofs to herald the arrival of a sheriff's posse.

But the hours sped by and the lawmen didn't come.

Rolf and Seth hung around the ranch yard, smoking incessantly. The other cowboy, a taciturn oldster by the name of Tom Week, came in from his job of clearing the few water-holes on the spread. He wanted chow, and Mary took it out to him in the bunkhouse. Tom Week, she felt sure, was not working in with Rolf and Seth, but it was not because he was virtuous. He was just indifferent, content to get along in his own groove.

The hot burning sun went down on the western horizon in its usual sudden manner. Rolf and Seth had the buckboard ready in the yard. They walked around with two guns sagging heavily against their thighs. Often they peered out over the sage-covered land to the distant butte which marked the turn of the trail, but no riders came along. Then it was dark, with only a suspicion of light glowing across the sky from a hidden moon.

The gold was hauled out of the cellars and placed on the creaking buckboard.

'Nigh to a thousand ounces in each box. Kinda heavy,' grunted Rolf.

'Reckon it could set a *hombre* up nicely,' said Seth slyly. Rolf's face was hidden under the shadows of his broad-brimmed hat. But he answered sharply:

'Yuh'll git yore cut! If yuh think yuh clever enough to figger out a good play, fergit it! The boss would git yuh – with lead! Reckon yuh ought to know thet.'

'I was only talkin'!' snarled Seth.

'Wal, quit talkin' an' git movin'. Yuh got the order from the boss – not me! Yuh know yuh got to meet two *hombres* with pack-hosses out by Pike's buttes. I'll go with yuh, jest in case yuh figger to risk yore goldarned neck by shooshaying with thet gold.'

'Yuh know I was only talkin'!' snarled Seth again. 'I know blamed well I got to meet them galoots wi' the pack-hosses. Them fellers are takin' the gold over the border to Pueblo, whar the boss has got buyers, I reckon.'

'Let's git goin',' snapped Rolf, and he threw his cigarette to the ground and carefully stamped on it, which was the universal custom in this parched land in summer.

The buckboard rattled out of the ranch yard and drove swiftly out on to the trail. At a curtained window, Mary Lester watched it go with a feeling of relief and yet another feeling of dread. For where there was gold, there was death, she knew. And more so with stolen gold.

The bunkhouse door stood open about three inches. Tom Week watched the buckboard leave, and his face showed no expression. But he had been curious enough to get up from his bunk.

Seth Mundy drove the buckboard, whipping the horse to full effort. Rolf rode behind on his steeldust gelding, a fine, broadchested animal.

As they left the cottonwoods behind and headed out across a rocky trail that led to the desert country which steadily encroached on the sparse grass of the Circle Four, a rider moved his horse carefully from the deep shadows of the big trees.

Clint Randall turned in his saddle and his keen grey eyes searched over the ranch buildings a few hundred yards away. Seeing no movement, he jigged his horse forward and went after the buckboard. Although the night had engulfed it, he could still hear the creaks and rattles of its springs.

He had spent the afternoon sleeping. He felt vastly better for it. While Sheriff Hoot Sampson had had a posse scouring the trails for signs of heavily laden horses, he had kept his own counsel. He had told the sheriff nothing about seeing the boxes at the Circle Four that afternoon. He had gone against his duty and his conscience, but he had kept grimly to certain intentions he had.

He had seen it clearly. The bullion had been taken to the Circle Four as a temporary measure because the sheriff's men were out everywhere looking for the bandits. Obviously it would stay there until nightfall. Clint had been so sure of his reasoning that he had calmly lain down and slept, leaving instructions for someone to waken him an hour before sundown.

There was one thing he did not want: he did not want a posse tramping over the Circle Four ranch house and throwing rough questions at Mary. He just did not want it, and he had stilled all other questions in his mind.

He rode on along the rocky trail, allowing the horse to pick its own way. The rattles of the moving buckboard drifted back to him across the silent terrain. He did not want to get too close. He wanted to find out where the stolen gold was going. More important than grabbing Seth Mundy or Rolf was the chance that he might get closer to the men who employed them.

For Clint knew, as did Hoot Sampson and others in Laredo, that many of the robberies and shootings were planned by some big boss. When Tad Lester had slipped up, he had been working on his own. There had been few slip-ups when the unknown boss planned. The man who hired the gun-happy rannies of Laredo could be any one of three or four unscrupulous, big-time men in town. There was Lansing, who owned the Bonanza Saloon. There was Tippett who did nothing but gamble and win at it. And there were others. But Hoot Sampson had not a thing on any one of them.

Clint rode on, his face shadowed under his pulled-down hat. He took a chance and left the trail and rode across sage and mesquite ground to a distant butte. He figured he could get closer to the moving buckboard this way and stay under the cover of the butte.

The rocky upthrust rose like an ugly sentinel into the dark sky. He sidled his horse round the cliffs slowly. Then he reined in his horse and patted its head so that it would not whinny.

He saw the buckboard drive past with the horse pulling the load at a trot. He figured the trip would not be a long one because Seth Mundy was using the horse up fast.

Some minutes later he had crossed to the cover of an adjacent butte. Grass was thinner here, and there was no occasional bellow from hidden cattle. Instead he heard a faint howl from a distant coyote.

The chase went on for some miles and then the terrain became jagged with towering buttes. These were known as Pike's buttes, after some old, crazy prospector who had worked a placer there. Clint jigged his horse well in the shadows of the rising cliffs. He had the buckboard well in sight with the aid of a faint glow of light from the horizon when he suddenly heard subdued voices.

He realized men were greeting each other. The buckboard had stopped moving. He edged his horse further down the bluff until he could go no further without leaving the walls of the butte.

He could see the flare of sulphur matches as men lit smokes. As his eyes got the range, he saw dark blotches which were horses. There were a number of riderless horses, and he suddenly knew they were pack animals. He saw, fairly clearly now, two other riders besides Rolf and Seth.

Clint eased out his rifle from the saddle boot. He vaulted to the ground and hitched the reins to a jagged spur of rock. He did not want a spooked horse leaving him.

He realized he could not get any closer to the

owlhoots. He would have to start shooting and get the gold back. The play had run as far as he could allow it.

He crouched behind a convenient boulder, away from his horse, and sighted carefully one of the new riders. He had no idea who the man might be in the dark, and he did not care. He triggered the Winchester.

*Crack!*

The steel-jacketed shell cracked the air. The distant rider in the gloomy night pitched from his horse immediately.

'Dead, I figger!' muttered Clint.

As the rannigans out yonder scattered with startled oaths, he let loose another careful shot. The rifle roared, sending echoes through the buttes. The shell whined and took another rider in the chest. Clint saw the dark shape topple slowly from the saddle with a dragging motion.

But by that time, just seconds after his first shot, the two remaining men had flattened into the desert sand. The pack horses had spooked and, snorting wildly, were galloping in all directions.

Colt flame spat from the distance, but Clint merely smiled at it. He was out of range of a six-shooter. He levered his rifle over the rock and searched for a target. All he wanted was the slightest movement of the flattened men out yonder in the dark desert. He saw a Colt lance flame, and he triggered at it immediately. As the echoes died away, he listened for a cry of pain, but none came. Maybe he had missed that time!

The horse hitched to the buckboard was rearing

wildly. In the faintly-blue light he saw the animal gallop away towards a rock-strewn defile. And then the gloom became too deep and the buckboard was invisible to him.

The Colts out ahead were silent now. Worse than that, he could not be sure he could see the two men. There were patches on the desert bed, but they might be rocks. They were lying with the immobility of rocks. Grimly, he waited and peered ahead, hoping for something to move.

But as the silence continued, he realized that the other two men had crept away across the desert bed, probably like snakes, moving on their bellies and taking advantage of the scattered rocks.

Clint went out, moving slowly and determinedly across the sand to the spot where he judged the two dead men lay. As he came closer, he knew the horses had all galloped away. He went on, rifle ready and finger itching the trigger. The slightest move ahead and the rifle would challenge it instantly with death!

But he came upon the two prone bodies without a shot or movement to startle him. He examined the first one. The man was white and a typical border ruffian. Clint did not know him. The man had the stamp of hired gun-hand written all over him. He was also very dead.

Clint found the second *hombre*, and he was a Mexican. Swiftly, he saw that the man was not dead. But he was dying and religious oaths sighed from his lips. Clint turned him over but the man's eyes were glazed and he could not recognize anything.

The sudden drum of hoofs caused Clint to drop to one knee and level the rifle. He thought he saw the dark shape of galloping horses far away against the deep black gloom of a rising butte, and he fired grimly. He emptied the rifle and stopped to reload. The hoofs continued to drum out and a horse whinnied in fright.

Evidently he had hit nothing!

He ran back for his own horse. He knew that the two men had crept away until they had caught up with the spooked horses. Now they were making their escape.

By the time Clint got to his cayuse and leaped into the saddle, the night had swallowed up the riders. He cursed, forgetting that he had done well to stop the owlhoots' play. He rode on across the sandy wasteland. Suddenly he heard the snorting of a horse in fright, the lashing of hoofs on rock and the intense rattling of a straining buckboard.

He rowelled his mount and, seconds later, saw the buckboard ahead. The horse was rearing and kicking. The big wheels of the carriage had jammed in a tight groove among some rocks.

There was nothing else to do but give up the chase for the other men, and calm the horse. This he proceeded to do. The animal quietened down after a while under Clint's expert hands. Then he manoeuvred the wheel out of the groove, and backed the buckboard out on to the sandy bed.

He examined the load. There were four long boxes, just as he had seen carried into the ranch house earlier that day. And they answered to the description Hoot Sampson had given him. Branded on one side was the legend: LAREDO GOLD COMPANY.

The weight of each box was enough. A thousand ounces of gold was heavy enough for one man to handle for normal working purposes. The boxes were, he knew, lined with metal to prevent loss.

He hitched his own horse to the rear of the buckboard and then climbed on to the box. He took up the traces and drove off. He came through the buttes with a rifle in one hand and the traces in another.

'Now what the hell do I tell Hoot Sampson?' he muttered. He would have to tell the truth as long as it left Mary Lester out of it. Of course, she could not remain unaffected if Rolf was pulled in to account for his actions. Did the buckboard belong to Rolf Lester? It seemed that Rolf and Seth had the luck of their kind, for they had not stopped a bullet in the recent gun-play, so far as he knew.

Clint drove down from the buttes and found the trail that led through the mesquite and sage to Laredo. He was glad when the horse found the well-defined trail. Driving in the dark was full of hazards. A horse could easily lame itself.

He entered Laredo, driving slowly down the main street where yellow light spilled from dozens of saloons and the noise of the honky-tonks drifted through the air. Cowboys from the outlying spreads were in town to carouse. Placer miners from the Rio Pecos river nearby were exchanging their gold dust straight over the counter for rotgut rye. The Irish railroad workers would be in to drink and fight. There were, of course, just as many hard-working traders, stern ranchers and railroad officials as well as gold miners who knew the value of living and working in the protection of a law-abiding community.

*Fever of the Colt*

Clint found Hoot Sampson at the office, a cigarette in his mouth, his hat on the desk and his boots off.

'Takin' it easy?' asked Clint.

'Yuh said it. Bin ridin' and stampin' round all day after them mangey railroad bandits. No trail no-how. Guess we was too late gittin' thar, but how'n hell we to know thar's goin' to be a hold-up? Railroad guards didn't see the bullion git away either.'

'Yuh kin stop worrying, Hoot,' said Clint dryly. 'I've got the gold outside. Git on yore boots!'

His announcement got Hoot's boots on in record time. In seconds they were outside examining the bullion boxes.

'Reckon thet's them! How come yuh got 'em?'

'Help me in with 'em, Hoot. Then I'll give yuh the play.'

They got the boxes inside the office. They were too big for the safe, and so Hoot locked them in one of the cells.

Clint told him that he had ridden out to the trail that went past the Circle Four ranch, and that he had found the buckboard being driven out into the desert. He told Hoot how he had killed two men who had been waiting for the gold.

'Who was the *hombres* takin' the buckboard out?' rapped Hoot.

'Reckon it was Rolf Lester an' his sidekick, Seth Mundy,' he said quietly.

'Lester, huh! Thet ranny! Jest like Tad – an' the old man fer thet! How come yuh was so lucky to jump on 'em? What made yuh ride out thar, son?'

'Guess I wanted to see Mary Lester.'

'Huh! Heerd yuh went over thar at midday. Wal,

yuh done fine, Clint. Reckon we'll see iffen we kin pick up Rolf Lester. But if I got the jigger he's workin' fer, I'd nail his hide to a barn door with pleasure! Thet's the feller I want!'

Clint had to wait in the office until Hoot got a man to guard the place. Then the two lawmen went out into Laredo's streets. They looked at the buckboard and got the liveryman at the back of the office to take it in charge.

'Maybe we could git some feller to identify thet buckboard as belongin' to Rolf Lester, huh?'

'If it's his, should be simple to pin thet on him.'

They got their horses and led them slowly down the street.

'Figger we'll look in the Bonanza Saloon. Won't take more'n a minute while we're passin'. Thet's Rolf Lester's spot these days, I've bin noticin'. Drinks too much for a young ranny. Heerd yuh had a fight with him. Want me to jug him fer it?'

'Nope.'

'Suit yoreself. Me – I'll be happy when thet young cuss is plumb dead. An' shore as hell thet's what he will be purty soon! Reckon we'll go on to the Circle Four from the Bonanza.'

The saloon was at its rip-roaring height when they entered.

'Shore like a drink myself,' grunted Hoot Sampson. 'But these galoots jest go plumb crazy fer more rye until they're topped to their blasted sombreros!'

Clint Randall was staring hard at the counter, taking little heed of the sheriff's words. Rolf Lester and Seth were there. They were propping up the mahogany unconcernedly. Clint walked in closer, and the other two men saw him. Clint noticed the tightness of their lips, although lines on their hard faces curved in a smile.

Sheriff Hoot Sampson shouldered up.

'Yuh rannies were out in the desert jest over an hour ago. D'yuh aim to come along quietly to the cells or what?'

'What in tarnation yuh talkin' about, Sheriff?' drawled Rolf.

'I'm talkin' about gold.'

And Hoot Sampson's gun came out as if by magic. The red-moustached sheriff could draw with the swiftest in Laredo. He had been sheriff for a number of years for that simple and sound reason.

'Yuh figger to come quietly?' snapped Hoot Sampson.

To back him up, Clint eased his Colt into the palm of his hand.

Rolf Lester allowed a smile to flit over his face. He uttered the short, sneering laugh which was characteristic of him. He winked at Seth Mundy and settled back comfortably against the bar counter.

The hubbub in the bar subsided a bit. But not altogether. Even gun-play was of no account besides the importance of drinking. But onlookers eased away from the sheriff and his deputy.

'Yuh got yore loop tangled, Sheriff!' sneered Rolf. 'We ain't bin out in the desert tonight. Not so thet we know about it!' And he laughed again.

Seth Mundy's lined, dirty face creased in a grin.

'Reckon yuh kin put thet gun away. Feller can't drink in peace. Don't know what this burg is a-cumin' to!'

Hoot Sampson's mouth became set unpleasantly. He looked down at Rolf Lester's boots, and then at Seth's.

'Yuh got desert dust on yore boots!'

The two rannigans made a pretence of staring at their high-heeled riding boots. Sure enough there was a coating of reddish desert dust.

'Wal, now, if thet ain't dust! Any feller here got desert dust on his boots? Sheriff doesn't like it!' There was a guffaw at Rolf's sally.

Clint flicked a grim glance at Hoot.

'Maybe these *hombres* don't know what it's all about,' he suggested gently.

'Yuh know blamed well yuh bin shootin' it out with Clint hyar!' hissed Hoot Sampson. 'We've got yore buckboard an' the gold thet was stolen from the wrecked railroad car this afternoon. I'm askin' yuh to come down to the office and answer questions. Yuh cumin'?'

'Nope,' said Rolf softly. 'We ain't bin out in the desert, an' this dust's bin on my boots fer days. Same as Seth. He likes dust – yuh kin see thet any time! Reckon yuh'd better ask Dave Lansing where we bin this past few hours, Sheriff, afore thet gun pops an' Clint has to put yuh in a hang-noose party fer murder!'

There was a movement through the crowd and Dave Lansing came close to Clint and the sheriff.

'These boys have bin playing cards all night,' he said easily. Dave Lansing was a burly saturnine fellow in a black gambler's suit. He wore a clean white shirt and black tie. His hands were soft and white. He wore a curt moustache which gave him an air of dignity.

'Rolf and Seth Mundy were in my little back room,' he elaborated. 'Been there all night. Other witnesses can swear to that!'

# 3

# MURDER IN THE STORM

Sheriff Hoot Sampson put his gun back in his holster with a very slow air of deliberation.

'Yuh really mean thet, Lansing? Yuh prepared to swear thet on oath?'

Dave Lansing had surprise on his suave face.

'Sure do! I tell yuh the boys have been playin' cards with me an' Secker an' MacBride over there!'

'Alibis!' snapped Hoot Sampson. 'Yuh got it all figgered out fine. Let's git, Clint!'

They turned without another word and walked through the crowded bar. On few faces was there any sympathy for the lawmen. Most of the rannigans who had watched the play thought the whole thing rather amusing. Few of them knew all about it, but the sheriff and his deputy had been made to look foolish, and that was good enough.

Hoot Sampson and Clint went back to the office and, at a nod, the other guard went back to his favourite saloon.

'Wal, at least we got the gold,' murmured Clint.

'Them fellers had it all figgered out!' grunted Hoot indignantly. 'An' me havin' to put my gun back! Thet Dave Lansing is shore a fine liar.'

'Shore is,' said Clint. 'Because it was Rolf and Seth I saw drivin' out with the buckboard. Maybe we kin trip Lester with the buckboard. Maybe we kin prove it's his.'

Hoot Sampson was frowning, puzzled.

'I don't git everythin' straight, Clint. Whar was the gold all the blamed afternoon? How come those two rannies were takin' it out into the desert at night? I had men out on all the goshdarned trails lookin' fer riders with thet gold.'

'Reckon they must ha' had it hidden,' said Clint shortly.

He was still grimly intent upon keeping Mary Lester out of it. If it were known she had helped the men hide the gold she might have to answer serious charges.

'Wal, the gold goes back to the Laredo Gold Company tomorrow,' returned Hoot. 'Hope they git the blamed stuff away this time!'

Not long after that they had a visitor to the office. He was Malcolm Starn, a freight-line owner in the town.

'I was in thet bar, Sheriff,' he began, 'and I saw yore play with them *hombres*. Me – I don't like Rolf Lester – or thet sidekick, Seth Mundy. What was wrong Sheriff? Anything I can do to help?'

Hoot Sampson looked at the medium-sized man in store clothes and shook his head. He liked Malcolm Starn well enough. The quiet man was not too talkative about his affairs, but he had a sound reputation. He was a man who did not drink a lot. He did not wear guns. He was often out of the town on business.

'It ain't much,' said Hoot Sampson. 'We've got the gold back thet was stolen from the railroad, an' we figgered thet Rolf and Seth had plenty to do with it.'

'Got the gold! Thet's fine!' and Malcolm Starn took out a little snuff-box and held it out invitingly. The others declined with a grin, and Starn took a generous dose of snuff.

'Glad to hear yuh're keepin' these gun-happy rannies in order, Sheriff,' he observed. 'Reckon I've lost out on some o' these hold-ups myself. Wal, reckon I'll git along. I've had my two drinks – enough for the night!'

Clint got to his feet.

'Jest a minute, Starn. Reckon yuh know all the buckboards round here. Jest come round to the livery fer a minute. Maybe yuh could look over a buckboard an' tell us who owns it.'

Starn nodded.

'Anythin' to oblige yuh lawmen. I reckon men in this town can't do business without law an' order. So I support yuh fellers. It's right enough – I sell most o' the buckboards round here. I kin tell yuh a lot jest by lookin' at a buckboard.'

'I figgered yuh could, Starn,' said Clint.

The three men went round to the back of the sheriff's office. With the aid of a lantern, Starn spent some time examining the buckboard which Clint had brought in.

'One thing's for shore,' stated Malcolm Starn. 'I didn't sell this buggy.'

'Kin yuh identify it as belongin' to Rolf Lester?' asked Clint grimly.

Starn did not hesitate.

'I can't say it belongs to him. Maybe it does, maybe it don't. But I didn't sell him it. An' I kin tell yuh, I supplied the Circle Four family with buggies for some time now.'

Clint nodded.

'All right, Starn. We'll jest keep at it. We might pin the ownership o' this buggy on Rolf Lester.'

'An' then the galoot will reckon it was stolen from him!' growled Hoot Sampson.

The two lawmen of Laredo returned to the office, and Starn went to his bachelor home behind his freight office.

'Look hyar, Clint, yuh'd better git some more shut-eye!' growled Hoot Sampson. 'Thet bit yuh had this afternoon ain't no use to a big *hombre* like yuh.'

Clint laughed, went up the stairs to the upper storey where he had a room. He took off his boots and hung up his gunbelts. He rolled on to the bunk and immediately fell asleep.

It seemed hardly minutes later, but it might have been an hour, when he was awakened by the roar of many Colts.

He jumped up, found his boots and buckled on his belt in swift, clear-headed motions. He moved quickly down the stairs to join an enraged sheriff.

'Goldarn this town! A man can't git any rest!'

The sudden crash of glass and the whine of a Colt slug made them scatter for cover.

'Broken the cussed window!' roared Hoot.

Clint had his two guns in his hands. Colts were

roaring all round the office. Another window tinkled as a slug went through. Clint listened intently for about half a minute.

'Reckon thar's three or four rannies shootin'!' he stated.

'What's the goldarned idee?' roared out Hoot Sampson. 'Ain't these jiggers got no use fer the Law? What's the idee o' shootin' up the sheriff's office?'

He was more enraged about the broken windows than any possibility of injury.

Clint moved to the gaping window in the office. He poked a Colt over the ledge and waited. Suddenly a gun roared and flame lanced momentarily, but it was enough for the deputy. He triggered instantly at the gunshot.

He heard a sudden howl of pain, and he grinned thinly. He moved away from the window in case some *hombre* outside was waiting to sight his gun flame. He left Hoot at the other window. The sheriff was snapping shots out into the darkness.

Clint went down the passage that led to the cells. At the end of the passage was a door which was seldom opened. It was bolted and barred. He withdrew the rusty bolt and took down the cross-bar. He slipped out into the back yard of the office building. On the right was the livery.

He got behind a water-butt and crouched. Across the way he could see the dim figure of a man standing close to the post supporting the false front of the nearby building.

Clint took careful aim and fired.

He saw the man spin ludicrously round the post and sink to the ground as if in agony.

Clint stepped swiftly across the way and crouched beside the man. The first thing that struck him was the strong smell of drink. The man was pretty well topped. Clint thought he knew the rannigan. He was a bar loafer who worked when money became tight with him. He could not remember the man's name.

Clint sidled along the boardwalk of the nearby building and stared across the road. There was a certain amount of light spilling from a saloon. And he could see a man hugging the wall of the building next to the saloon. Clint waited until the man poked a long-barrelled Colt round the corner of the wall.

Clint moved his own gun and sent death crashing across the road. The man staggered backwards under the impact of the heavy slug. He fell to the ground and squirmed ominously. Then he lay still.

There was sudden movement, as if the last man to die had been a signal. Horses' hoofs drummed all at once. A horse snorted nearby. Suddenly two men rode big mounts out of the alleys opposite the sheriff's office and desperately rowelled the horses into a full lope.

Sheriff Hoot Sampson appeared at the office main door, and he emptied his guns at the fleeing horsemen.

'Darned gun-totin' rannigans!' he roared.

If his horse had been saddled, he would have ridden after the men. But his horse was in the livery, and there was not time to get it.

Clint knew the play was over. He went along to the men he had shot across the road. Again he looked at a typical gun-wearing border ruffian. He looked the type of hard-bitten galoot who could be hired for any unscrupulous purpose. Clint let him drop back to the ground with sudden distaste.

He rejoined Hoot Sampson at the office door. One or two punchers had emerged from the saloons, now that the shooting had died away, and were staring curiously.

'Reckon this is jest a boothill town,' declared Clint. 'I'll go along and tell the town grave-digger we got two dead jiggers fer him.'

'Is this town civilized or ain't it?' fumed Hoot. 'We got a railroad and a telegraph. We got the chance to make Laredo a fine town. Thar's good range even if it's a bit dry right now. Thar's gold. Everything to make a mighty fine town. An' what do we git? A lot o' durned gunslingin' gents who figger thet all we got hyar is theirs jest fer the shootin'. I wonder what the heck they wanted to shoot up the office fer?'

'Jest hired gun-men,' stated Clint. 'I shore would like to know who the fellers who got away were. An' I figger they were after the gold, Hoot.'

'Iffen we'd been killed, the Texas Rangers would ha' moved into this town,' said Hoot Sampson with conviction. 'Thar's still plenty o' law in this country. How the heck did those rannies expect to git the gold?'

'Wal, if we were shot to hell, four riders could take a box up on each hoss,' said Clint dryly. 'Maybe thet was the idea. Or maybe those fellers jest got orders to shoot us to hell!'

Two men strolled over to give critical inspection of the bullet holes in the office building. One man was Dave Lansing, from the Bonanza Saloon, and the other was Doc Hawton, a quiet, studious man with an

unsmiling expression. Both men wore store clothes
and did not look like rangemen.

'Shore seems yuh're gittin' unpopular, Sheriff!'
drawled Lansing. 'Why all the shootin'?'

'I wouldn't know.' snarled Hoot, and he stroked
his bristly red moustache. 'Go git back and git yoreself an alibi, Lansing!'

The other continued to smile. His dark eyes swept
over the office building.

'Guess the taxes will be high in this burg next year
to pay fer the damage!' he observed.

As he strolled away, Doc Hawton shook his head in
despair. He hooked his fingers in his vest and spoke
sepulchrally.

'I hear there are more dead men! There is too
much violence in this town. Every day I am dressing
wounds. There is too much of it.'

'Good fer business, Doc!' snapped Hoot, and he
turned and went back to his room.

After Clint had got the grave-digger to heave the
dead men away, he went back to his bunk. This time
he went to sleep with his guns on. It was not so
comfortable, but maybe it was safer.

The next day the gold was deposited with the officials
of the Laredo Gold Company. The mine was in a
canyon just off the Rio Pecos river. It was a new
company and the gold was coming out well. Many of
the town's leading traders were share-holders.

Clint found time next day to ride out to the Circle
Four. As he came over the sage and mesquite, he
became aware of signs of a rising wind. The sky was a
brassy colour and unclouded. But the wind was press-

ing steadily in one direction. He felt sure the velocity was increasing.

When the ranch house came into view, he urged his horse into a canter and rode quickly into the ranch yard.

He saw no sign of Rolf or Seth. A few minutes later he was talking to Mary on the front porch. She closed the door behind her uncompromisingly. Her face was set.

'What do yuh want?'

'Lissen, Mary,' he said sternly, 'I know all about the gold bein' here yesterday.'

'Yuh knew?'

Her set expression wavered and she looked suddenly helpless.

'I saw the boxes being taken in by Seth,' he said harshly. 'An' I followed them out into the desert thet night. We kinda swapped lead an' two men got killed. It might have bin Rolf.'

'Why do you tell me this?' she whispered.

'I jest want yuh to know I'm here to help yuh, not hound yuh down,' he said briefly.

'Yuh're here to pick up Rolf!' she accused.

He smiled wryly.

'Nope. Yore brother got himself a nice alibi last night. A gent by the name o' Dave Lansing swore Rolf and Seth were in a back room o' the Bonanza Saloon playin' cards all night. So Rolf and Seth have witnesses to prove they weren't out in the desert. Thet's the kind o' game yore brother is playin', Mary.'

'Does the sheriff know about the gold being here?' she whispered.

'Nope. I kept thet to myself. So don't give yoreself away.'

She stared past him, across the mesquite grass-covered land. She sensed the rising wind.

'Yuh'd better go afore Rolf an' Seth come back,' she choked.

'I jest want to say this, Mary. Someday Rolf is goin' to git what he deserves. He's goin' to sling lead too offen. I want to be able to help yuh when thet happens, Mary. An' don't let Rolf make yuh do anything agin the law – anythin' yuh'll be ashamed of.'

She was staring anxiously at the trail where it rounded the solitary butte on the Circle Four range. Then:

'Yuh'd better go – quickly! Here's Rolf!'

Clint Randall turned slowly. He walked down the steps to the dusty ranch yard and waited until the other man rode up. Rolf Lester swung down from the saddle and stamped over, a sudden grin of triumph on his face.

'I don't like yuh around here, feller!' he snapped.

'Maybe yuh'd like to take off yore belt like yuh did the other day?' observed Clint Randall dryly.

Rolf uttered his short sneering laugh.

'Now ain't thet a right good idea!' His confidence was so assured. He knew he had beaten Clint the other day. Inwardly, he gloated over the prospect of doing it again. And this time there would be no inter-fering rancher to prevent Clint's gun-hand from being smashed up. Rolf unhooked his holster belt and slung it over a nearby fence.

'You can't fight here!' cried Mary Lester, in alarm.

Clint unbuckled his own belt and was slinging it over the fence when Rolf swung a wicked left hook.

Clint moved his head in a swift effort to dodge, but the blow rammed home. He backed and shook the pain out of his head. Then he advanced with angry determination to smash this young buckeroo. The last time Rolf had had it all his own way, because of the tiredness that had permeated Clint's bones.

Clint's arms rammed out with the iron-strength of a mechanical piston. Bones rasped on Rolf's chin. Then the other man barged in, ignoring the first few blows. His arms hacked through the air, through Clint's guard and hammered home at the body. Clint swung more blows, like a steam hammer that never tires. He saw a split appear on Rolf's cheek and blood oozed. Then a rock-like fist staggered him and he went back against a fence.

Rolf grinned and drew his fist back for a pulverising blow. But Clint bounced from the springy fence and two fists ploughed into Rolf's eyes, dazing him and causing him to falter. His fist swung out mechanically, but missed because Clint sidestepped.

Clint bored in with renewed determination. He just flung fists as if he was trying to knock down a tree. Rolf staggered back for some time, and they went across the ranch yard in this fashion. Mary followed helplessly.

Clint was not the man to forget that Rolf had beaten him in a fight once. He hated the recollection. It was the grim desire to establish himself that drove him to ram blow after blow into Rolf's face.

The sound of harsh grunts and slithering boots drifted over the ranch yard. Rolf Lester, knowing he was being slowly but grimly beaten, tried a few rough-house tricks. He slashed out with his boot more than once, but Clint avoided the kick. He bored in again and landed two punishing punches that drew harsh panting sounds from Rolf.

Rolf backed up against a fence and threw out arms that moved slowly because of the dull haze that clouded his eyes, Instinctively his arms moved like hard bulwarks, trying to ward off Clint's slow, savage punches. Then he began to slither down, with the fence supporting him. Clint knocked the man's face around some more. Rolf's eyes closed and then jerked open in an effort to keep his senses. His mouth was open and twisted as he gasped for breath. One arm was hooked around the fence, though he hardly knew it.

Clint rammed fists into the man's mouth and eyes unmercifully. With every slamming punch, he felt grim, stern satisfaction. He did not intend to relent until the tough young buckeroo had tasted savage punishment.

He did not see Seth Mundy ride into the yard. The man dismounted and approached with a gait which was almost creeping.

Seth pulled a gun and stuck it in Clint's back.

'Yuh kin quit the rough play now!' he rapped.

Clint stepped back with heavy movements, like a big man who is tired after a terrific effort. Rolf Lester hung on to the fence and fought the mists that sick-ened his brain. Then, laboriously, he dragged himself up, swayed and instinctively wiped the blood from his mouth.

Clint eyed the dirty-looking Seth Mundy.

'Yuh kin put thet gun away. Yuh're stickin' it into a deputy.'

'Mebbe. But deputies ha' bin shot to hell afore!'

They did not realize that Mary walked swiftly out of the ranch house with a rifle. She knew how to use it and she came near to them.

'Yuh can put that gun away, Seth Mundy!' she said clearly. 'And you can get off this ranch, Clint Randall. I won't have yuh fighting with Rolf!'

He smiled thinly at that.

'Sorry yuh had to see it, Mary. But I owed that to Rolf. Seems we kinda dislike each other.'

'For goodness sake get on your hoss!' she cried. 'And ride out of here. There's too much trouble, Clint Randall, following you!'

Seth Mundy had slipped his gun back into his holster and turned away muttering. Clint walked to the fence, got his gunbelt and buckled it on. Then he strode along to his horse. He climbed into the saddle and rode away without so much as a backward glance.

He had told Mary about knowing the gold had been in the ranch house. He had told her he wanted to help her, and he had asked her not to do anything she might feel ashamed of later. More than this he could not do. He had plainly shown he was her friend.

And there had been some satisfaction in smashing Rolf Lester. That the young fool would hate him more than ever, he did not doubt.

He began to notice the velocity of the wind again. It was howling round some distant buttes. The air was already gritty. If the pressure increased, a sand storm would blow up.

He rode another mile and realized the sand storm
was upon him. Dust and grit was tearing through the
air and visibility was hazy. He looked up more than
once from the cover of his bandana and could see
nothing but the driving screen of yellow sand. His
horse plodded on, reduced to a walk. Sand stung his
face continuously.

He realized the sand and dust was blowing in from
the arid land further east and would settle on the
sparse vegetation of the Circle Four spread and choke
it up. If this process went on, there would come a time
when the Circle Four would be arid land itself. That
had happened in the valleys that surrounded Laredo.
It was a continual fight against the encroachment of
the desert.

He hunched in the saddle and let the horse plod
on. He reckoned he was still another five miles from
Laredo. He was on the trail, but he could not recognize his surroundings.

He hoped the storm would blow out, but he had a
fair idea it might increase in velocity yet. If it did, he
would have to seek shelter. As it was, the five miles to
town would be rather a struggle for the horse.

Rider and horse braced against the harsh wind
and plodded through the never-ending screen of
sand. All at once, above the howl of the wind, Clint
heard the sound of Colt fire ahead. He thought he
saw the stab of flame in the glaring yellow air, but he
was not sure.

And then, as he urged his horse on, he came upon
an extraordinary scene enacted in the swirling storm.

He saw a man rise from the ground and grab at a
horse. Everything was indistinct. Another second and

the man disappeared in the driving sand-filled air. He seemed to be urging his horse fiercely.

After progressing another yard or two, Clint found a man lying across the trail. He was dressed in rough clothes such as a tattered vest and dirt-stained trousers. He did not seem to be a cowboy. There was no horse nearby. Apparently the animal had run off.

Clint dropped from his horse and, holding the reins examined the man. There was a bullet wound in his chest, but he was not dead. Grimly, Clint knew it would be only a matter of time before he was. There was little he could do for the man, beyond propping him up so that blood did not run into his mouth.

The man opened pain-filled eyes, and seeing Clint began to jerk hoarse, spasmodic words.

'Fogel . . . shot me . . . taken my gold . . .'

The man coughed and choked horribly, and his words ceased. Then:

'Fogel . . . rode with me . . . down . . . the trail . . . said he was goin' . . . to . . . join up with . . . big boss . . . in . . . Laredo . . .'

That was all, for the man went limp with startling suddenness. Clint knew he was dead.

He laid him down. In this buffeting storm there was little he could do. He could not bury him; for the storm was spooking the horse and the animal needed a firm rein. Clint put a foot in his stirrup and mounted. He urged the horse on, scrutinising the outlines of the trail with eyes that felt raw with the scouring sand.

The man's words were firmly implanted in his mind.

A man named Fogel had shot the man and taken his gold. Evidently the dead man had been a placer miner, although the trail he had been riding was a long way off the Rio Pecos river. The man called Fogel had ridden along with the other man until he had shot him – presumably for the gold. Fogel was going to join up with a big boss in Laredo.

The last bit of information excited Clint's brain. The big boss was the man who employed Rolf Lester and Seth Mundy and others in Laredo. This unknown boss had hired the gunhands whom Clint had killed out in the desert when the gold had been driven out by buckboard. The same unknown man had hired the gun-happy *hombres* to shoot up the sheriff's office. He was behind a great deal of activity – all lawless – and yet he contrived to remain unknown to the sheriff and his deputy.

Apparently the unknown boss was to receive a new ally in the man called Fogel.

Clint made a mental note to watch out for the killer.

The ride back to Laredo was hardly a pleasant job, but he made the town after more than an hour's struggle against the sand and air. When he rode down the main stem of the town, awnings were flapping under the pressure of the storm. No one was on the streets. Clint pressed on until he reached the sheriff's office. He walked the horse into the cover of the livery and left the animal there, still saddled. He went to look for Sheriff Hoot Sampson.

He could not find his side-kick in the office, so Clint came out again, locking the door behind him.

Clint Randall was a young fellow and no solitary

*hombre*. He liked to find his friends in a saloon just like any other man. Leaving the office, he thought he would look in at the Bonanza Saloon. He might see Jesse Teed or old Doc Hawton, with his humourless talk. Well, at least the Doc was no killer or gun happy border ruffian! Or he might come across Hoot Sampson. The sheriff should be somewhere.

Clint walked through the batwing doors and immediately saw Doc Hawton. The quiet old fellow was fond of a glass of rye, although he was never drunk.

'Howdy, Doc!'

Doc Hawton turned. 'Howdy. I see you are seeking shelter from the storm!'

'Yeah. I jest rode through it, coming down from the Circle Four. Found a dying man on the trail, Doc.'

'Another body!' exclaimed the Doc sepulchrally. 'This town will soon be one large boothill!'

Clint laughed.

'Have a drink. It ain't as bad as thet. Always plenty o' decent folks in any town. It's always the bad *hombres* who make the most noise and attract attention. Take Laredo. It's a mighty fine town. Gonna be an important centre if it keeps on growin'!'

Dave Lansing walked up to them. There was a smile on his dark face.

'Hello, gents! See you figure the Bonanza is the safest saloon in town when a blow is on!'

'All the same to me,' declared Clint.

'Is thet so? Wal, I don't figure thet at all. I figure the Bonanza is the finest saloon in town – better than the Gold Nugget or the Last Chance. See they got a new manager at the Last Chance. The feller jest rode in an' took over.'

Doc Hawton glanced up. He was much smaller than Dave Lansing.

'A new citizen?' he inquired in his studious tones.

'Is thet what you'd call him?' Dave Lansing laughed. 'I heard his name was Fogel.'

The one word tensed Clint's interest.

'How come this stranger got the job?' he asked.

Dave Lansing stared back.

'Yuh're asking me somethin' I know nothin' about. All I heard was the jigger rode in out o' the storm. Reckon he had papers of introduction because Winter, the old manager, made no bones. Old Winter is goin' to live with his married daughter on her ranch.'

'Reckon we'll mosey along to the Last Chance,' said Clint. 'Yuh comin', Doc?'

'Not in this storm, Deputy. No, sir. Sand in the throat can cause many bodily ills.'

'Reckon I'll go along all the same,' and Clint grinned at the old Doc and left him with Dave Lansing.

As he lurched through the storm outside, he wondered about Dave Lansing. He had suspected him of being the boss who employed Rolf Lester and other lawless men. He had suspected him of engineering the railroad holdups, and so had Hoot Sampson.

Dave Lansing had been ready to provide Rolf Lester and Seth Mundy with alibis the night they had ridden out of the desert! Now why? Why the heck did he do that?

The dying man had said Fogel was going to join the big boss in Laredo. Those words could be interpreted many ways. A big boss might be anybody. On the other hand, with a lawless customer, the big boss would surely be the unknown organiser of banditry. But if this man, Fogel, had taken over the managership of the Last Chance saloon, how did that tie up with the big boss? Who owned the Last Chance?

Clint wondered if Dave Lansing owned the Last Chance. It would be a good idea to make inquiries.

Clint made his way down the road and found the Last Chance batwings. The storm seemed to be losing its intensity. He could walk upright without leaning on the wind!

He entered the saloon and moved up to the counter. Due to the storm, the place was pretty full. Men in range garb propped up the mahogany and argued and drank. No one took any notice of Clint Randall.

He soon found Fogel. The man was behind the bar counter studying some ledgers. His study was pretty perfunctory, for he suddenly pushed them to one side with a cynical laugh.

He was a big, dust-covered man in riding clothes. Whatever he might be, he was certainly not a saloon manager by profession. He wore a large Stetson even in the saloon. He had two Colts slung on his thighs. His black shirt rippled with the big body inside. He was wearing leather riding chaps which even now were covered with the dust of a long ride. Clint studied the man without showing his interest. Unless the dying man had been crazy, Fogel had cold-bloodedly shot him and made off with his gold. So the man was a killer. The two Colts backed up that impression.

Fogel had a bold sort of face, with dark, amused eyes and a permanent cynical smile.

'A dangerous *hombre* if ever I saw one!' muttered Clint. No one in the saloon took much notice of Fogel except the bartender who showed the man some of the stock. Then he called Fogel 'Bert' once or twice and Clint heard it. So that was the fellow's full name apparently.

Clint came out of the Last Chance and thrust through the diminishing storm until he reached the office. He went in and found Hoot Sampson slowly writing out some records.

'I've bin lookin' at the new manager of the Last Chance,' announced Clint.

'Yeah? What's he done?'

'Wal, he killed a jigger out on the trail and took his gold.'

Hoot raised bushy eyebrows which were as red as his moustache.

'You ain't jokin'! I ain't heard o' the feller.'

'Reckon he's the latest addition to Laredo's gun-happy *hombres*.'

Hoot stopped writing.

'How come yuh know this?'

'Wal, I was riding through the storm – I'd bin over to the Circle Four – when I heard a shot and found this dying rannigan. Reckon he was a miner. Told me a *hombre* named Fogel had robbed him and shot him. Then he said this Fogel was goin' to join up with the big boss in Laredo.'

'The big boss!' echoed Hoot Sampson.

'So I find this Bert Fogel taking over the Last

Chance. He ain't buyin' it. He's the new manager. Say, Hoot, d'yuh know who owns the Last Chance?'

Hoot fingered his bristly moustache.

'Now yuh ask I can't say rightly thet I know who owns it. Old Winter bin manager thar for some years. Maybe Dave Lansing owns the place.'

'Reckon I'll have to find out,' said Clint. 'Because maybe the *hombre* who owns the Last Chance is the big boss who is behind these robberies.'

'Wal, now, yuh might git the information over at the county building. They got all records o' land an' property in this town.'

Clint nodded. He was determined to find out who owned the Last Chance Saloon. It might be a false alarm or a small point that had no real value, but he would look into it.

# 4

# HELL-BENT GENTS

Because it was not a matter of haste, Clint Randall waited util the storm had blown out before he set off for the county building. Like most sand storms, it reached a peak of intensity and then quickly subsided.

Clint walked down the main road, noting the piled up drifts of sand. Already men and women were busy cleaning up, shovelling the unwanted sand to vacant ground. The sun blared down like an orange-red globe. The rest of the day would be hot. It was always hot in Laredo.

He entered the County Building and saw the clerk. Soon the records of land claims and property assessments were placed before him. He quickly traced the owner of the Last Chance Saloon.

The man who owned the property was Malcolm Starn! Thoughtfully, Clint left the building.

He wondered why Malcolm Starn should employ a man like Bert Fogel. He wondered what situation had arisen that enabled a man to ride in and take over the managership of a saloon. For Bert Fogel was obviously a gun-man.

If the dying miner could be believed, Fogel was joining up with the big boss. But in reality, who had Bert Fogel joined up with? He was now actually working for Malcolm Starn if the ascertained facts meant anything.

It seemed a regular mix-up. Clint expelled his breath impatiently. He much preferred action to speculation.

He discarded the idea of going along to Malcolm Starn and asking him about Bert Fogel. If Starn had anything to hide, he certainly would not reveal it in answer to a few questions.

Clint had a hunch that it would be better to leave the situation the way it was. He would give Hoot Sampson the results of his small amount of investigation.

'That feller Starn has his finger in all sorts o' businesses,' growled Hoot Sampson after Clint had given him the facts. 'He's pretty shrewd. But I can't figger it out why he should hire this Fogel *hombre*!'

'We'll give them a little bit of rope,' decided Clint. 'I ain't forgettin' thet ranny killed a man. I'm a-goin' out to git the body. There ought to be a slug in it. A slug is a mighty good bit o' evidence sometimes.'

'Yeah. If yuh kin find the gun thet shot it, Clint.'

Clint Randall was as good as his word. He rode out down the trail that led east of Laredo and kept keen eyes open for sign of the dead man.

He knew the killing had taken place about a mile or so from the Circle Four, and so he had some sort of location. But it needed a lot of searching before he finally found the body. It was partly covered with drifting sand, which had saved it from the buzzards. A few wheeled slowly like black shapes in the sky.

He unearthed the body and heaved it over his horse. He mounted behind and rode back to Laredo as the sun mounted high in the heavens. As he entered the outskirts of the town, Mexican children and chickens played in the dust outside shacks. A few men stared at the deputy riding with the body, but none stared long.

Clint got Doc Hawton to come along to the sheriff's office and do a bit of surgery in extracting the bullet. He wanted Doc Hawton as a witness that the slug had been taken from the body. Soon the man would have to be buried. Plenty quick, Clint decided with a grimmace. It was too hot for dead bodies in Laredo.

The slug was a .44 fired from a long-barrelled Colt.

'One or two scratches on this slug,' said Clint, examining it with a magnifying glass, 'We might prove it came out o' Bert Fogel's guns – iffen we ever git the chance to examine thet feller's hoglegs!'

The grave-digger was sent for and the body taken to Boothill. Like many rough-living, illiterate miners, there was not a document on the body to identify it. He was just one more dead man.

Clint and Hoot Sampson, as single men, were having a meal in the Chinese eating-house later. A few hours had passed since the dead miner had been buried. The heat of the midday sun was less now. They had hardly got through their jerky beef and beans when a rider careered up the street, leaped from his horse and dashed into the restaurant.

'Hear yuh were here, Sheriff!' he bawled. 'Thar's

bin a hold-up down at the Laredo Gold Company. Right down by the Rio Pecos river.'

Hoot did not stop eating. But he gulped at his beef and then jumped up.

'Nuthin' but darned hold-ups!' he roared. 'Let's go!'

There was some delay. They had to get horses and saddle them. It was this inevitable delay that always helped the robbers.

The rider was a hired hand from the gold company and his name was Sam Jansen. A few minutes later the three men were riding furiously in the direction of the Rio Pecos, towards the canyon in which the Laredo Gold Company operated.

They got some account of the hold-up from Sam Jansen.

'Three fellers jest rode in and grabbed bags o' dust!' he bawled as they thundered over the arid roll of land. 'They was wearin' bandanas over their faces. Couldn't see nuthin'. Jest rode in and grabbed the dust out o' the assaying office. Kilt one man who figgered to shoot at 'em.'

'Did no one git an idee who the cusses were?' shouted Hoot Sampson.

'Nope. Might ha' bin anyone. Had hats pulled down over their danged eyes. I seen them ridin' out. Three men from the gold company set off ridin' after 'em. One man was the manager.'

'Maybe they caught up with the jiggers?'

'Nope. Thet's what we all figgered, but only two men came ridin' back. Them robbers had shot one feller – one o' the guards we got. Thet's when I set off fer town.'

'Wal, them robbers shore got plenty o' start!' grumbled Sheriff Hoot Sampson. 'All we kin do now is aim to pick up their sign.'

Clint smiled grimly. He knew they were too late to get within shooting distance of the robbers.

Hoofs pounded the semi-arid land. The aroma of sage floated through the dust laden air. As they neared the canyon, the waterless land was covered with cholla, ocotillo and a dozen barbed desert growths interspersed with towering saguaros. Then the three riders turned lathered mounts off the desert and entered the canyon which lay parallel with the Rio Pecos river. Here mesquite and grama grass grew in tufts, but there were no cows to take advantage of the grazing. Instead the log buildings of the Laredo Gold Company squatted on the reddish sand, shale and grass. The buildings were stout, made from cedar logs which had been floated down the river from the hills where the trees grew.

As the three riders galloped in, there were two other mounted men waiting for them.

'We're ridin' out with yuh!' shouted John Filby, the mine manager.

The other burly man was a hired guard. The horsemen rode off in a cloud of dust, heading for the other end of the canyon.

'Those galoots shot one of our men!' bawled John Filby. 'The cusses plugged him in the guts, an' he was losing so much blood we had to turn back with him to save his life.'

'And they killed another feller at the start, too!' commented Randall. 'Thet makes 'em right nice *hombres*!'

John Filby was able to take them right out into the desert to the spot where they had had to turn back with the badly wounded guard. But the robbers' trail showed clear ahead. Horses' hoofs had dug deeply at the sand. The trail showed clear ahead for miles.

The ground was fairly firm, and they went along at a good canter. As the miles went by and they followed the sign, they knew the bandits had ridden for Pueblo, the Mexican town over the border.

'Once they git in thet hell-town, how kin I git 'em out?' grumbled Hoot Sampson to Clint as they rode side by side.

Clint nodded. He knew the Mexican town was simply a rendezvous for every lawless *hombre* in the district. There was another point, too. Sheriff Hoot Sampson had no power over the border. Pueblo was not in his bailiwick.

Hoot knew that and was disgusted.

'These goldarned thieves ha' got me on the prod all the time! Dogblastit! All I ever do is chase around!'

They rode into Pueblo some two hours later, parched men and lathered horses. The adobe buildings of the town huddled together. It was a ramshackle hell-town, and no one of any respectability lived there. Naked children played in the alkali dust and *vaqueros* in steeple shaped hats lounged and sprawled in the shade of a few wooden porches.

'Shore stinks!' grunted Hoot Sampson.

The party rode slowly down the dusty main stem.

A few wooden cantinas stood here and there amid the adobes. Dark-skinned *vaqueros* watched the riders warily.

'Mex town!' grunted out Hoot Sampson. 'Wal, we've lost those *hombres*. No one round here will give 'em away. Let's halt it, fellers.'

He reined in his horse and the others followed suit. The sheriff leaned heavily on his saddle horn and wiped the sweat and dust from his face with a red bandana.

John Filby glared around the ramshackle town.

'I swear those hellions weren't Mexicans! Those three bad *hombres* were white!'

'Yuh'll find a few white renegades in this dump,' interposed Clint.

It was rather amazing – as if his words bad been some sort of prophecy – but even as he spoke, the blistered batwing doors of a cantina swung and three men walked out on to the plank porch. They moved slowly and leaned lazily against the clapboard walls of the building. They began to make brown paper cigarettes, and then lit them.

Clint Randall found himself staring at Rolf Lester. Next to him was the dirty Seth Mundy. The third man was more than interesting.

Bert Fogel casually lit his cigarette as if the sheriff of Laredo and his men out there in the street did not exist!

'That's our meat!' growled Hoot Sampson suddenly.

He was out of his saddle before he realized afresh that this town was not in his jurisdiction. But that did not deter Hoot Sampson from speaking his mind.

'I ain't goin' to bandy words with you jiggers!' bawled Hoot. He strode up to the lounging men on the porch. 'I reckon yuh jest rode into this town less than an hour ago. I figger yuh're the galoots who robbed the Laredo Gold Company. I can't prove it. But by Gawd, I'll remember it!'

'You goin' loco with the heat?' sneered Rolf Lester. 'We don't know what the hell yuh're talking about!'

'This is Mexico, Sheriff,' grated Seth. 'An' we bin here all day.'

'What doin'?' snapped Hoot.

'Aw, jest drinkin'.'

'Yuh'd be topped to yore blasted sombrero if yuh'd bin here all day drinkin'!' snapped the sheriff.

'Yuh been here long, Fogel?' asked Clint.

He knew he would not get a straight answer, but there would be some grim amusement in extracting a reply from the man.

'Nope. I jest rode in and met up with these gents. I'm new to these parts.'

'Shore. I hear yuh takin' over the Last Chance Saloon. Yuh like thet business?'

'Yeah. I like it!' drawled Bert Fogel, and there was amusement in his dark eyes.

'Do yuh know anythin' about the robbery?'

'Not a blasted thing, Deputy. You figger I look like a robber?'

Fogel's hands hovered above his Colt butts. Clint thinned his lips. He stared back at the man. He knew Fogel would not be fool enough to go for gun-play. He had nothing to gain by it. But the rannigan was certainly a robber. He had killed the miner in the sandstorm, and robbed him of his gold. Now he had apparently linked up with Rolf Lester. Hadn't the dying miner said Fogel intended to link up with the big boss? Rolf Lester and Seth Mundy were in the pay of this boss.

Hoot Sampson tramped back to his horse and leaped to the saddle.

'Let's git!' he snapped. 'We can't pin anything on these jiggers, an' they know it.'

'By thunder, they kill a man —' John Filby swore sulphurously.

'We'll git them in the act some day!' rapped Hoot. 'Then they'll git plumb riddled wi' lead!'

'In the meantime, they git free!'

'Allus another day!' growled Hoot.

The horsemen rode slowly back through the alkali dust of the main street.

'Thet Fogel *hombre* is jest another gun-man,' rumbled Hoot Sampson, as he rode alongside Clint. 'Yuh don't have to tell me what he is. I kin see his ornery character plenty plain.'

'I don't git the tie-up with Malcolm Starn,' said Clint.

'Nope. Pretty queer, thet.'

'Starn must know somethin' about this feller,' mused Clint. 'He must know the type of *hombre* he is employin'. I don't git it.'

'Dunned fast mover, too,' grunted Hoot Sampson. 'He ain't bin in this territory more'n a few hours an' he kills a man and takes his gold. Then he fixes up wi' Rolf Lester and helps rob the Laredo Gold Company.'

Clint reached out with one arm and gripped Hoot as their horses cantered close together.

'Look, I've got some kinda idee in mind I'd like to play. I'm ridin' back to Pueblo.'

'I'll play it with yuh.'

'Nope. I've got a hunch I kin play it better alone.

You ride back to Laredo afore them bad *hombres* figger to start somethin' else.'

Clint wheeled his horse and applied spurs. The animal crow hopped at first and then sprang into a full lope. Clint headed back across the desert for the ramshackle Mexican town.

He had nothing more than a hunch. He just wanted to get near to Rolf Lester, Bert Fogel and Seth. His hunch centred around Bert Fogel's guns. One of those big, low-slung Colts had killed the unknown miner. The slug from the miner's body had not hit a bone and had therefore not spread. It could be proved to have come from one of Fogle's guns – if they could get the right gun for examination.

That was the extent of Clint's hunch. Nothing more.

He rode back into the first few adobes and shacks and then hitched the horse to a tie-rail. He walked slowly, with long strides down the dusty road, passing somnolent Mexicans lying on the plank walks. There were a few frowsy *senoritas* beside the tin shacks, and naked children played in the alkali with the chickens, dogs and goats. There was not much activity. It was too hot for anyone but gringoes to walk about.

Clint approached the cantina where he had last seen Rolf Lester and Bert Fogel. He stopped in the shade of a porch and watched the cantina. Three horses were tied to the hitching rail. He recognized the big roan as belonging to Rolf Lester's remuda. The other two animals were wiry ponies such as were used a lot on most ranches.

Even as Clint lolled inconspicuously in the shade of the porch beside three velvet-jacketed, dozing

Mexicans, a rider cantered his horse round the corner of the road and came down to the other three horses at the hitching rail.

The man dismounted, hitched his horse and walked very slowly into the cantina.

He was a medium sized man in store clothes. His black suit was powdered with the dust of his ride.

Clint knew him. The man was Malcolm Starn.

# 5

# DEATH AT THE RAILROAD

Clint figured it was time he took a look into the cantina. He walked quickly across the road and moved quietly to the sun-blistered batwing doors. He stopped there. He could see into the dim interior. He could hear voices, too. As his eyes became accustomed to the comparative dimness within, he saw Malcolm Starn standing near to three other men. Raucous laughter suddenly swelled out.

Rolf Lester and his two side kicks seemed to be enjoying some joke.

Clint walked in suddenly. He was at the counter before the others were aware of him.

He looked at them steadily, grimly, and their laughter ceased.

'Howdy, Mister Starn!' Clint greeted the other calmly.

Malcolm Starn seemed to stiffen. His lean, small-ish face tightened into set lines.

'Howdy, Deputy!'

The half-breed bartender moved up, stared at Clint.

'Red-eye,' said Clint, and he smiled at Malcolm Starn. 'You drinkin'?'

'No. I – I don't like likker this time o' day!'

'Wal, I ain't askin' yore pals,' declared Clint, and when the bartender placed the raw whiskey in front of him, he drank it quickly.

Rolf Lester shot an amused glance at Bert Fogel. Clint saw the look. He gathered that Rolf had taken a fancy to Bert Fogel. They were birds of a feather, but Fogel was the more experienced ruffian of the two. Rolf Lester simply had the conceit and red guts of a wild young rannigan.

'Thought yuh rode back to yore own bailiwick, Deputy?' drawled Rolf.

'Don't think,' advised Randall. 'It kin lead to mistakes. Fer instance, I figgered yuh and yore pals robbed the Laredo Gold Company and shot two men. But thinkin' ain't provin'.' Clint turned to Malcolm Starn, stared into his set face and said 'Yuh heard about the robbery at the gold company?'

Starn nodded.

'Shore. I heard before I rode out.'

'I figger these rannigans did it!' And Clint waved a hand to the other three.

But he was watching Starn. The freight-line owner showed no surprise or any other emotion. Taunt lines etched deeply into his face, as if he was determined to maintain a poker face.

Rolf Lester's rough laugh echoed through the empty cantina. 'As yuh said, feller, thinkin' ain't provin'! I reckon yuh're boring Mister Starn. Time

we livened things up in this burg.' It had been Clint
Randall's intention to gain a hint as to why Malcolm
Starn had ridden into Pueblo. Clint thought Starn
knew where to find Rolf Lester and the others. The
whole thing was rather strange, but Starn's poker
face had given nothing away.

Suddenly Rolf Lester whipped his hardware from
leather. The guns barked. The long barrels were
pointed at Clint's boots. The slugs tore into the
planks. Gunsmoke hazed up before Clint's eyes. The
guns exploded as fast as Rolf Lester triggered.

'Dance, yuh nosy snake!' bawled Rolf.

Clint Randall never moved.

His feet stood square on the boards. As the slugs bit
all around, he never moved an inch. His hands hung
by his side, only inches from his guns. His grey eyes
were riveted on Rolf Lester's sneer-twisted features.

Then the chambers on the bull-like young
buckeroo's guns were empty. The last slug thudded
into the planks. The last explosion died away. Only
the gunsmoke remained.

The moment Rolf's guns were empty, Clint
whipped his sixguns from his holsters. He seemed to
scoop them out with incredible speed. Rolf's guns
were empty. Fogel and Seth Mundy were beaten on
the draw. Bert Fogel's hands stopped inches from his
gun butts. It was as well he stopped, for two heavy
Colts were staring at his heart.

'Now Mister Starn, yuh kin help the law,' snapped
Clint. 'Rolf had his little play. Take them hoglegs
outa them holsters, Mister Starn. An' if yuh happen
to pack a little hidden Derringer, keep it hidden. I
kin beat yuh on the draw.'

'I assure you I have no gun, Deputy,' muttered Malcolm Starn. 'And I want to help the law. I believe in the law —'

'Wal, git the guns!'

Clint had his eyes on Bert Fogel's pearl-inlaid Colts. Malcolm Starn took the guns from the holsters. He moved slowly, pulling the guns out and backing away each time as if the men might grab at him. Clint watched him warily. He was not sure of Malcolm Starn any more. The man was employing Bert Fogel as a manager of the Last Chance. He had ridden into the Mexican town to meet the gunman. Was Starn behind the robbery of the gold company? It seemed incredible.

The freight-line owner placed the hardware on a table. Clint moved over. He put one of his guns back into the holster. He picked up the two pearl-studded Colts and held them in one capable hand.

'Mighty fine work, Mister Starn,' he murmured. 'Now iffen we could only git the gold these hellions took outa the gold company's offices, we'd shore pin murder on them.'

'Yuh can't pin thet on us!' snapped Rolf Lester. 'Yuh won't find no gold!'

He had found plenty of pleasure in trying to make Clint Randall dance like a fool, but he saw no humour in the present situation.

'Reckon yuh must ha' bin met by some rider,' snapped Clint. 'Yuh ain't foolin' no one, Lester. Three fellers robbed the gold company and killed one man and badly wounded another. Them jiggers headed this way. We ride up an' find yuh lot hyar. It shore adds up.'

'Thet's jest yore suspicious mind, Deputy,' drawled Bert Fogel.

'Yeah, I got a suspicious mind – where yuh're concerned!' flashed Randall. 'Adios, *amigos*! Enjoy Pueblo's rotgut while yuh got the chance! I'm agoin'. Comin', Mister Starn? Or ha' yuh got business with these gents?'

'I'll come with you,' said Malcolm Starn quickly.

'Wal, git them hoglegs. I don't want a slug in the back. We kin drop these guns in the road. It'll give these fellers some honest stoopin' to do pickin' 'em up!'

But Clint did not tell Bert Fogel that his guns would be examined under a magnifying glass.

The freight-line owner gathered the hardware and walked out of the cantina with Clint. Malcolm Starn got to his saddle and rode down the street to where Clint had tied his horse. The three men on the porch of the cantina watched them with grim sneers.

Clint Randall and Starn rode out into the desert in silence. Starn still held the guns. Clint did not fear the man. After a while he turned to him.

'Yuh kin throw them irons into the dust now, Mister Starn. Maybe them *hombres* will ride out fer them and maybe not. I don't kinda care much.'

Malcolm Starn complied with the other's request and then he glanced interrogatively at the pearl-handled weapons.

'Yuh keeping them?'

'Yeah. I got reasons. These shooters are .44 barrelled. Ain't so many around nowadays. Mostly .45.'

He did not tell the other that he was trying to prove

that Fogel's guns had fired the slug that killed the unknown miner. The slugs that had killed and wounded the men in the robbery of the Laredo Gold Company would be .45 and it would be almost impossible to prove that Rolf Lester or Seth Mundy had killed and shot the men. .45 guns were so numerous that nothing could be deduced from proving that a .45 slug had killed the gold company man. But it was possible to trace the owners of .44 weapons in Laredo, and the owners might have alibis. The killing might be narrowed down to Bert Fogel. It was just a chance.

'Those guns are Fogel's,' said Malcolm Starn slowly.

'Yeah.'

'You know thet man is workin' for me now, Randall.'

'Yeah. How come yuh hired him?'

'I wanted a strong galoot for the Last Chance. Thet saloon is gittin' kinda lawless. I'm a firm believer in law and order, Deputy.'

Clint wondered why Malcolm Starn was so insistent upon his love of law and order.

'Yuh didn't know much about the *hombre* when yuh hired him?' queried Clint.

'He was recommended to me. The other manager wanted to retire.'

Clint nodded. He saw the other had provided an answer for everything.

'Iffen Fogel is workin' for yuh, Mister Starn, I ought to tell yuh he's a bad *hombre.*'

'Maybe he's a bit wild,' said Starn slowly.

'Wild and pizenous. I ought to tell yuh I aim to keep an eye on him.'

'Maybe I ought to watch him, too.'

Clint sat erect in the saddle, stared at the heat haze shimmering over the hard-baked gypsum sand.

'Maybe yuh kin tell me how come yuh rode over to Pueblo to see them hell-bent gents, Mister Starn?'

'I jest rode over,' said Malcolm Starn harshly.

'Yuh knew they'd be thar?'

'I knew Fogel was there. I only wanted to see thet *hombre.*'

'Business?'

'Yep. Business,' said Starn grimly.

Clint saw he was getting nowhere fast with the man. But he did not worry about it. Clint wore a serene smile on his bronzed face.

'Wal, I aim to git them *hombres* fer a hangnoose party some day, Mister Starn, so yuh ought to cast around fer a new manager right now. The hellion yuh got mightn't last long!'

And then Malcolm Starn said a strange thing.

'Why don't yuh put yore peepers on Dave Lansing!' he burst out. 'He's —' He checked himself as suddenly as he had broken into words.

Clint watched him, warily, but Malcolm Starn compressed his lips and rode on in silence.

'Yep, Dave Lansing is a mighty smooth feller,' Clint said eventually. 'Mighty smooth. We're shore watchin' him. Anythin' yuh know about thet feller?'

'Not a thing,' said Malcolm Starn harshly.

At that he fed steel to his pony and hit the trail for Laredo. Clint followed, his big bay taking everything in its stride. They came into town as the sun sank on the horizon and the distant hills were already bluish in the evening light. Clint rode up to the sheriff's office and stabled his horse. He went in the office, boots clumping on the boards, and found Hoot Sampson at the back of the sheriff's office, locking a *loco* Mexican in the hoosegow. Hoot came back as the crazy man yelled abuse. They went into the office and shut the door.

'Run amok,' grunted Hoot. 'Now what yuh got thar?'

Clint placed the pearl inlaid guns before him on the desk. They lay on top of bills of wanted men and other notices.

'Bert Fogel's hoglegs.' said Clint with a grin.

Hoot Sampson's red eyebrows jerked up.

'Gawd a'mighty! Yuh shore git what yuh go after.'

Clint gave all about seeing Malcolm Starn. Hoot Sampson's hard eyes were puzzled at the end of it.

For Clint there was an hour's work examining the guns and the slug taken from the body of the dead miner. He had no equipment beyond a strong magnifying glass. After the initial inspection he knew the slug had been fired from the .44 gun which Fogel would wear in the right-hand holster. The side of this gun was smooth where the weight of the gun lay against the owner's thigh. It was undoubtedly a right-hand gun. And it had fired the slug that killed the miner.

To prove it, Clint fired a shot into a sack of corn in the stable. He got the slug and compared it with the one that had killed a man. Both slugs had identical scratches which showed strongly under the magnifying glass. The barrel of the gun had caused the scratches. No other .44 gun would mark a slug exactly the same. And there were few .44 guns used in this territory. Clint spent some time making diagrams, and then he was done. He put the evidence before Hoot Sampson, and the tough, grizzled sheriff knitted his brows as he studied the work.

'Yuh got sometin' thar, Clint,' he grunted at last. 'But I can't say I like this kind o' evidence. We can't string the hellion up on thet. We got to put him afore the Judge. I shore like to ketch a jigger red-handed with plenty o' witnesses!'

'We won't act yet,' said Clint. 'We kin wait. This evidence will keep. I reckon thet Fogel *hombre* will hang himself and his pals if we give 'em enough rope.'

He put the drawings, the slugs and the guns into a safe and locked the door. Then he and Hoot went out to the Chinese eat-house. They left the crazy Mexican singing mournful songs in Spanish.

They had a good tuck-in at the eating house. There was one thing about the Chinaman's chow – there was plenty of it for a hungry man. They each had a hunk of hot pie, lavishly surrounded by beans. Mugs of coffee steamed beside the plates. They finished with molasses and milk bread. Hoot Sampson wiped his mouth on his gaberdine shirt sleeve.

'Not bad! Yer figger a feller oughta marry a Chinese, Deputy? Seems the only way a jigger kin git regular chow.'

'Kinda better iffen he married a woman,' returned Clint.

Hoot shot him a look from under his bushy eyebrows.

'Yeah. Now I heerd thet Mary Lester kin cook real

fine. When yuh goin' to do anythin' about thet?'

'This ain't the best o' times,' said Clint with a faint grin.

They walked slowly through the dusk to the office. As they opened the door with the key, a man sidled towards them. He had been waiting in the darkness of the gable end.

'Sheriff! I want to talk to you!'

Hoot and Clint turned.

The man was Tom Week. He stood with a graven face, but he was plainly uneasy.

'Shoot,' declared the sheriff.

'Not hyar. I don't want to be seen. Let's git inside. I bin waitin' fer yuh.'

'We bin gittin' chow. Yuh could ha' asked fer us.'

'Didn't want to ask no questions.'

The taciturn oldster slipped into the office as soon as the door swung in. The other two followed. They went into the office proper, and before Hoot could get the lamp burning Tom Week began to deliver his message.

'I ain't no gun-toter, Sheriff. I minds me own bizness. I jest go on workin' fer the Circle Four like I used ter. But I bin seeing things. It ain't none o' my bizness, either. But I got it figgered to tell yuh.'

Hoot lit the lamp, turned curiously to the other. 'What's bitin' yuh, old-timer?'

'Yuh'd better git alawng to Crag's End wi' a posse,' said Tom Week unhurriedly. 'Thar's a loco coming in tonight and thar's a gang aimin' to derail it at Crag's End.'

'Spill it!' snapped Hoot. 'How come yuh know this?'

'A lot o' jiggers met up at the Circle Four ranch house. Maybe they figgered I wasn't around – I dunno. But I heerd. I heerd Rolf tellin' thet lazy skunk, Seth Mundy, jest where they figgered to derail the loco.'

'What the blazes is on the railroad this time?' snapped Hoot.

'I didn't hear. I jest skedaddled and got my horse. There was plenty o' them gun-totin' breeds from Pueblo an' a new feller wi' Rolf and Seth.'

'Fogel,' commented Clint. He was already reaching for a Winchester. Rapidly, he filled his belt with steel-jacketed shells. He had plenty of Colt ammunition.

'Must be gold – or maybe a payroll!' jerked Hoot.

'Thet train is bound to be comin' in this time o' night, so it'll be the payroll.'

'Banker's money, too,' snapped Hoot. 'There's a lot o' beef in the town's corrals. Bet yuh tha's money arrivin' to pay for thet beef.'

'How's Mary?' Clint asked quickly. 'She know about what's goin' on?'

'Rolf locked her in her room.'

Clint's eyes clouded with sudden anger. A sudden idea bit his mind but it would have to wait.

Clint went to the livery to get horses saddled. Hoot ran over to the Cattlemen's Association office and found two men there. As ranchers with a stake in the stability of the town, they responded immediately. One went off to get more recruits for a posse. The other returned to the sheriff's office, taking his horse with him. Hoot was wise enough not to go near the Bonanza Saloon. He did not want it spread around town that a posse was setting off. That might tip the bandits. The leader might be in town.

Hoot Sampson rounded up four other tough men who had served as deputies before. He swore them in in exactly five seconds dead as they walked back along the darkening road. Sometimes Hoot was a stickler for ceremony.

The posse rode out of town two at a time and without any noise. Once out of town the leaders cantered their horses and soon the other riders came up in a thunder of hoofs. They were a mile or two out now, with the deep silence of the night thickening all around. As the eight grim men bunched up together, and hoofs cut the ground, the aroma of sage drifted up with the dust. The horses pounded across grassland, now yellow with the summer heat and lack of rain, but the riders could not see the grass. They trusted to the horses to keep a sure footing. There were jackrabbit holes, chunks of rock and shale to test the horses. Night riding was always unsafe.

To Clint, as he threw questions and got replies from the other men, the set-up became clear. The incoming train carried a safe full of currency in bills. Some of the money was for the banks and the other for the well-paid workers in the gold mines.

He knew all about Crag's End, of course. The railroad wound through some rocky country six miles away, skirting the imaginary Texas-Mexico border. The track led through numerous defiles. A train could easily be halted or derailed there.

Rolf Lester had slipped up in overlooking the self-effacing Tom Week.

One of the possemen knew the train's schedule. There was no time to lose if they wanted to get there in time to stop a derailment.

Away to the west the river wandered over its rocky bed, and so the terrain nearby was not desert. The horses did skirt occasional clumps of grease-wood and chaparral, but mostly the land was sage and mesquite. Dust rose as hoofs thundered the earth. Eight riders hunched low in the saddle, feet firmly stirruped as they swerved with the galloping horses.

As the dusk thickened, a moon peeped out from behind thin, drifting clouds. They were not rain clouds, but wispy streaks of cottonwool which drifted idly by, month after month.

The posse rode into the rocky country and had to slow and let the horses find a way with safety. There were red, crumbling bluffs on all sides.

They rode on until they came across the double track running across the flat land. On either side of the line, the nimble horses plonked iron-shod hoofs down unerringly between timbers.

They entered the first rocky defile. The line turned through the rocky bluffs on either side.

Clint and Hoot were in the lead and as they urged the horses round the bend they saw moving figures a few hundred yards away. The two lawmen pulled the horses up and jigged them close to the overhanging bluffs. The rest of the posse piled up behind.

'We want one man to ride ahead – round the rocky pile-up and try to stop the train afore she gits this far,' said Clint.

Hoot nodded. 'That's right. Who's it gonna be?'

One of the ranchers volunteered, and at a nod from Hoot he wheeled his horse and rode away to the left of the line. He would find a trail through without cutting into the holdup men. As the man rode away, Hoot nodded.

'All right. Let's work round them jiggers. Seems like they're pilin' some rock on the line. Git all round 'em, an' let 'em have some hot lead.'

The riders urged the horses further down the defile and then some rode the animals up into steep ledges and paths fit only for deer or goats. But they wanted to spread out.

Clint found himself with two possemen. They rode up a difficult cleft in the side of the defile, and then dismounted, hitching the horses to some tough cactus plants which had roots yards deep. Even if the horses spooked, they would stay put.

Then Clint and the men moved forward, rifle in hand. They scrambled quickly to positions above the men working at barring the railroad line.

Then, all at once, a rifle shot snapped through the night air.

'Some feller ran into the holdup men!' snapped Clint.

The possemen flung themselves forward, jerked rifles over the edge of the bluff and selected targets.

The men on the track were still standing in uncertainty when hell burst loose. Clint's rifle roared with others, and two shadowy figures on the line staggered and crashed to the ground.

Rifles spat from the other side of the defile as some men tried to run for cover. Two more men spun round with the impact of a bullet ploughing into them. They fell to the ground and one cursed in pain.

From the boulders that lined the railroad cut,

answering fire proved that a number of holdup men had been hiding while the others barred the line. The shrill whinny of spooked horses denoted that the robbers had mounts hidden.

Clint used his Winchester on the bursts of gunfire that flashed from the boulders near the line. In the pale moonlight, much of the shooting was touch and go. There was the danger of friend shooting at friend. Guns boomed from all quarters. Clint waited for more gun-flashes, but none came. As he peered down into the defile, he wondered if the holdup men had been all shot up. He did not think so. But there was a sudden silence. Once a rifle cracked from high up on the other side of the railroad cut, but that was all.

Then, all at once, the sudden clatter of horses' hoofs further down the defile indicated an attempt at getaway on the part of the ambushed holdup men.

At the clatter of hoofs, rifles roared instantaneously. Down the defile a bunch of shadowy riders seemed to leap out of the rocks and spur the animals madly. The riders were low in the saddle, but as the rifles cracked and boomed two men fell as the horses were hit.

The animals fell and kicked in terror. The other riders were madly jerking figures disappearing round the bend of the defile. Shots tore after them until they vanished. They had the luck of their breed, for not one more man toppled.

The possemen scrambled down to the flat bed of the railroad cut. They ran for their horses. Clint was one of the first to spur his animal down the line. He rammed the rifle into the saddle boot, and crouched low to the horse's neck.

In seconds he encountered the two writhing horses that had belonged to the holdup men. The horses lay across the line. Clint reined in with the idea of using a bullet on them to end their torment.

He never even got his hand near his gun.

A man lurched drunkenly from the rocky hiding-holes in the side of the defile.

Clint saw the flash of his gun. Even as it blinded him, he jabbed cruel spurs into his mount.

The animal sprang and reared in fright. Hoofs pawed for the dark sky. The movement saved Clint's life. A slug whistled past his Stetson. It had been destined to smash him between the eyes. Death would have been nasty, but quick. With superb horsemanship, Clint hung on while his right hand scooped at his Colt. He threw the roaring slug at the lurching holdup man even as the fellow levelled his shooting iron for another shot.

Clint's shot dug into the man and he dropped his gun instantly. He clawed at his guts and staggered forward, out of the shadows.

Clint saw the man was Seth Mundy. He had been lurching because he had been wounded previously.

Seth Mundy lurched on and then sprawled his whole length across the railroad line. He died hard, with great rasping gasps coming from him.

The other possemen were crowding behind Clint now. Only one of them had so far stopped a bullet. Clint pushed his hardware back into leather.

'Put them hosses outa misery, some feller,' he shouted, and he rowelled his horse. The cayuse sprang into a full lope and continued down the line after the escaping remnants of the holdup gang.

The dull clatter of hoofs rose in a steady, ominous drum as the posse rode down the double set of lines. The defile turned twice like a snake. It was this twisting that had aided the escape of the bandits. They had got out of sight plenty quick. The posse thundered along the flat bed of the defile for almost a mile without any sign of the holdup gang. Then the terrain on both sides of the track levelled off into flat shale and brush country. The posse spread out and thundered across the plain.

The owl-hoots had gone. They had turned off the line and the night had swallowed them.

But the posse rode on until they came to the halted train. The rancher who had ridden out ahead had succeeded in halting the train by means of a small fire on the track. Steam tossed from the locomotive as the engineers looked down at the posse-men. There were armed guards in the car carrying the bullion. A few passengers had stuck their heads out inquiringly.

'Yuh kin take her in now!' yelled Hoot Sampson to the engineer. 'The line is clear. We got rid o' them holdup agents. But take it easy. How fast does this heap travel?'

'Reckon we kin move up to twenty-five miles an hour,' bawled the engineer.

Hoot rubbed dust out of his red moustache and stared up at the hissing steel monster.

'Gawd a'mighty, thet's too fast fer man to travel! Yuh take it easy – understand?'

Some minutes later, with a mournful wail from its hooter, the locomotive began to heave its load forward. With a clank and hiss, the train moved on.

The posse rode back, through the defile, behind the train. Clint and Hoot stopped to examine the dead men who had been laid to one side. Neither Rolf Lester nor Bert Fogel were among the bandits. Hoot recognized one or two gunmen border breeds who had given trouble in the past. The others were unknown renegades – probably from the Mexican town across the border.

Clint stopped to go through Seth Mundy's pockets in the hope that the man might carry some document or provide some clue as to the organiser of the holdup. But there was nothing. He had not expected anything much. Men like Seth Mundy could hardly read, anyway.

'Thet's the end o' his trail then!' grunted Hoot Sampson. 'Aw, let's git back to town. Maybe some other hellions are kicking up a shindang by now!'

But before they hit the town, Clint spoke out.

'I'm agoin' over to the Circle Four. I jest don't like leavin' Mary Lester out there with those rannigans. Ain't much I kin do, but I shore want to go over.'

'Yuh ought to git thet gal up before the preacher!' grunted Hoot.

'I got my loop kinda tangled jest now. I killed her other brother, an' I'm workin' on Rolf for a hang-noose.' Clint smiled ruefully. 'Shore figger the odds are stacked agin me an' Mary ever hittin' it off.'

He left the sheriff with the other riders and wheeled his horse over the flat terrain towards the distant Circle Four. The six miles went under the hoofs of the strong bay, and he slackened the cayuse to a walk as the ranch buildings loomed through the ghostly moonlight. The cottonwoods, with their white lint, were absolutely motionless. There was not a breath of air. There was deep silence all around, broken only by a distant coyote who howled from some crag at the moon. Clint rode slowly into the ranch yard and threw the reins over the corral poles. He stood still for some minutes and lit a cigarette which he rolled. He watched the light from the ranch house window. The wooden shutters on the outside had not been closed but a blind obscured any view of the inside.

He wondered if Rolf had returned, and figured he would find out pretty quick.

Taking a last draw on the brown-paper cigarette, he dropped it into the dust and ground it with his heel.

He walked slowly forward to the porch steps.

He had no plan. He was not quite sure what he wanted. He was just like any other young man who is worried about the girl who means a lot to him. He just wanted to see Mary, reassure himself.

He rapped on the door firmly, and after a few moments, heard footsteps. They sounded like they were a man's high-heel riding boots. Mary was not coming to the door. That was not surprising in a lawless country late at night.

The door opened, and Clint found himself staring into Dave Lansing's saturnine face – and a gun!

Suddenly Dave Lansing smiled.

'Why, hello, Deputy! This ain't my house, but I guess I kin ask yuh to come in.'

The owner of the Bonanza saloon put his gun down by his side. He was wearing his black suit, white shirt and black tie; his trousers were tucked into riding boots but he had no holster.

'What are yuh doin' here?' demanded Clint, as he strode into the house.

'Jest visiting,' murmured Lansing.

They entered the big living room, with its Indian rugs and large stone fireplace. The night was cooling and a fire had been lit.

Clint came face to face with Mary Lester and Rolf. Dave Lansing put the gun down on the top of a black oak dresser as if he had merely picked it up for the purpose of coming to the door.

Clint searched the girl's face. He saw at once the trace of past tears.

'Hello, Mary. Are yuh all right?'

'Shore she's all right!' rasped Rolf Lester immediately. 'Why the heck shouldn't she be?'

Clint turned a set face to him.

'I figgered she might be worried and upset.'

'She ain't. What's she got to worry about?'

'You. Yuh bin out with the gang thet was all set to rob the train tonight. Yuh're bull-strong, Rolf Lester, to take on two jobs in one day.'

'What's all this about the train?' asked Dave Lansing quickly.

'A holdup gang tried to derail the cars. There was currency on board. But it didn't come off. Some fellers got shot instead.'

Mary's eyes were wide with controlled, inward terror. Clint went on grimly.

'Whar's Seth Mundy ?'

'In town, I reckon,' snapped Rolf. Clint spoke the words quietly to Mary.

'Seth Mundy is dead. I put a slug in him myself. He was killed trying to hold up a train.'

Her hand went to her mouth and she shook her head helplessly as if the words were terrifying.

'Yuh know Seth ain't in town,' snapped Clint, turning to Rolf Lester. 'An' yuh were with him an' the rest of the outfit.'

Rolf Lester's blue eyes were bright with fury.

'Ef yuh must know, I ain't bin out o' this ranch house tonight!'

Clint refused to answer. He merely stared at the other's unholy, hate-filled blue eyes and knew he was lying.

Rolf's lips twisted in a savage smile. He turned his head to Dave Lansing.

'Ain't thet right, Dave? Where have I bin tonight?'

'With me – in this house,' said Dave Lansing quietly. Rolf smiled uglily, and his blue eyes gleamed up to Mary as she stood staring at Clint.

'Ain't thet right, Mary? Where we bin tonight?'

'In this house,' she answered automatically.

Clint just looked at her. She evaded his eyes, and stood motionless as if the lie had hurt her like a blow.

Clint took out the makings and rolled another cigarette. He worked leisurely and just waited. The silence was deep in the house, and then Mary seemed to sob and she turned away and sank in a large rocking-chair.

'Yuh know darned well yuh were with thet holdup gang,' said Clint evenly. He flicked his grey eyes at Dave Lansing, who stood near the oak dresser. 'Thet's the second time yuh've alibied Rolf. What d'yuh git out o' all this, Lansing?'

Dave Lansing smiled.

'Don't you believe me – and Mary? The three of us ιa' bin here all night.'

'Yuh'll be tellin' me thet Seth Mundy was here all night soon!' snapped Clint.

Dave Lansing shrugged and retained his imperturbable smile. Rolf glared as if he wanted to use a gun. Mary sat in the chair with downcast eyes.

Clint blew out smoke and said thinly: 'I hope yuh know what yuh're doin', Rolf, bringin' all this trouble on Mary.'

'We ain't in trouble.'

Clint eyed him narrowly. There was something strange about the way he sat in his chair behind the table. It was not like the bull-headed Rolf Lester to sit still while the man he hated intruded in his own home.

'Yuh ain't in trouble?' queried Clint, and he moved suddenly.

He strode round the table and gripped Rolf Lester by the shoulder. He pulled the big young buckeroo round in his seat. Rolf made a last-minute attempt to resist, but too late.

Clint saw the blood-soaked bandage wrapped round the man's arm.

He had been hiding the wound under the table.

'So yuh got plugged!' rapped Clint.

'Yuh jump fences too quick!' sneered Rolf. 'I shot myself jest an hour ago. It was an accident!'

Clint went to the door, hard-faced.

'Yuh're two mighty smart *hombres* – but watch yore steps. I got a hunch yuh're bent fer Boothill!'

# 6

# TROUBLE IN THE DESERT

Clint rode his bay back to Laredo as the kerosene lamps made patches of yellow light in the main street. He was tired of riding and grimly sick of the events which kept him from Mary Lester's side. He got to the stable at the back of the office and put the bay to feed and rest.

He let himself into the office with his key, and found Hoot Sampson was out, so went straight upstairs to his room and washed the trail dust from him. Standing only in his pants, he sluiced cold water over his body. He felt better after putting on a clean shirt, and buckling on his holster belt again, checked the guns, filling the chambers with new brass shells.

He went out into the dusty main stem and found his way to the Last Chance. The saloon was bursting to capacity. There was plenty of money going over the mahogany, some of it in the form of gold dust which placer miners had won out of the Rio Pecos.

Clint figured he could do with a shot of whiskey.

He set his eyes on Bert Fogel, who was standing behind the counter with an amused look on his dark face and eyes. The man was dressed in brown trousers and black shirt which rippled tight across his chest. He was not working but had a glass of whiskey in his hand, and seemed to consider he was something of an ornament to the place, while two other bartenders coped with the incessant demands for more drink.

Clint caught his eyes.

'Whiskey, Mister Fogel, if yuh please, an' make it the best. I don't like rot-gut!'

Bert Fogel came over with the bottle and a glass. Clint put an old silver dollar on the mahogany.

'Yuh bin attendin' to business all night?' he asked.

'Yeah, more or less.'

'Maybe I'll ask the customers if yuh bin here all night,' murmured Clint.

Bert Fogel's eyes glinted cynically.

' 'Course, I gotta office at the back. In this job I got to make out bills and keep books. I've bin doin' thet tonight.'

'Bit of a change from gun-totin'!' said Clint.

The man's eyes glinted back at him.

'How come Starn picked on yuh for this job?' asked Clint bluntly.

'Ain't thet my business?' Fogel grated back at him.

'Shore. Jest curious, feller.'

Clint went out of the saloon and tramped the length of Laredo's main stem. He turned a block and found what he was looking for.

There was a legend above the false-fronted building.

MALCOLM STARN FREIGHT COMPANY

Clint knew Starn had a home at the back of the office. He knocked on the front door and waited.

He had to knock three times at minute intervals before he realized his knocks were not going to be answered.

He left the front door and on a hunch walked round to the back and stood in an alley formed between buildings.

He just wanted to speak to Malcolm Starn about Bert Fogel. He wanted to try to get something out of the freight-line owner. The blind covered window went dark, as if someone had suddenly extinguished a lamp.

Clint walked across the road and stood under the dark shadow of a false-front hotel and waited. He was just obeying instinctive hunches. There was something queer in the light going out as he knocked. Was Starn lying doggo?

Clint waited a long time, and the light wasn't turned on again.

He was about to turn away when he heard the creak of an opening door. He stayed in the shadow another minute.

He sensed more than saw a man leaving the back door of Starn's place. Clint crossed the road with long, swift strides and was beside the man before the unknown realized it.

Clint put out a detaining hand and gripped the man by the wrist.

He heard the exclamation of pain, and then saw the man's face. It was Malcolm Starn.

Then Clint withdrew his hand and look closely at it.

He smelled the blood even as he saw the stickiness on his hand. He glanced keenly at Malcolm Starn's wrist. It was bandaged and soaking with red blood.

'How did it happen?' rapped Clint.

He got the answer he expected.

'I had an accident, Randall. Shot my wrist with a doggone .45.'

'Thought yuh never used a gun?'

'No more I do. But I got to lookin' at a weapon I keep in my office. Then the durned thing exploded.'

'Did yuh git the slug out?'

'Nope. I bin bandaging the wound myself.'

'I'll take yuh along to Doc Hawton,' said Clint crisply.

They walked along and roused the doctor from his game of poker with a bosom friend. Malcolm Starn got his wound attended to while he repeated his story to Doc Hawton.

Clint did not believe a word of it!

This was the second *hombre* that night who had had accidents with a gun.

Clint just did not believe it.

He left Malcolm Starn with the doctor. He figured there was no way of talking a man into telling the truth if he did not want to.

On the way back to the office, he pondered over the events. Had Starn some stake in the robberies that went on? Had he been wounded in the rataplan down by the railroad? There was no need to wonder where Rolf Lester had got his wound. But how had Starn got his?

There was no answer except conjecture. Clint went to bed that night and forgot all about it. Conjecture was all very well, but in the rough-and-ready West, only seeing and believing had any reality.

The next morning, as they went out for eats, he told Hoot Sampson how he had found Rolf Lester at the Circle Four with Dave Lansing.

The Chinaman welcomed them as regular customers and set out the eggs and bacon.

'Dave Lansing plays a tricky hand!' growled Hoot. 'How come thet *hombre* is so ready to alibi Rolf Lester? And Mary Lester lying to save her no-good brother! Aw, doggone it. I figger we'll ketch up with them rannigans one fine day an' either fill 'em with lead or string 'em up!'

'Maybe we'll cotton on to why Starn hires Fogel,' added Clint. 'An' maybe we find out how he got thet wound.'

They were in the stable tightening the cinches on their horses when someone darkened the patch of light at the door.

Clint wheeled around.

Mary Lester was outlined in the doorway. She was wearing blue jeans and riding chaps, blue shirt with one button open at the top showing a bronzed, slender throat, and wore a new Stetson on her honey-coloured hair.

'Mary!'

With two long strides he was beside her. He searched her eyes.

'Why are yuh here?'

He saw the trouble clouding her blue eyes. She

had the blue eyes of all the Lesters, but unlike Rolf,
her eyes were not full of his unholy callousness.

'I – I wanted to see yuh!' she faltered.

'Kin I help yuh?' he urged.

She nodded. For a moment she seemed reluctant
to speak; then: 'Rolf and a man called Bert Fogel are
ridin' south today. I want you to stop them, Clint.'

'I'll do anything to help yuh,' he said quietly.

She seemed subdued and saddened.

'What are they doin' ridin' south?' he queried.

'I overheard,' she choked. 'They're goin' to meet
the boss and bust into a placer mining camp lower
down the Rio Pecos.'

'Gold again,' muttered Clint.

She nodded wearily.

'Yes. This camp is more'n twenty miles away – a
place called Monument Valley.'

'What do yuh want me to do with Rolf?' he asked
harshly.

'I want yuh to stop him ever getting to the camp!'

She laid a hand on his arm. Her eyes were appeal-
ing.

'How come Rolf kin ride? Ain't his arm botherin'
him?'

'He's so hard – he – he wouldn't let that stop him.
I'm not supposed to know yet that they are going.'

'Was Fogel at the Circle Four this morning?'

'Yes. He came over early.'

'Don't let the grass grow under thar feet!'
muttered Clint. 'Have those galoots set off, Mary?'

'Yes. They'll be on the way now. You'll have time to
catch up, though.'

Hoot began to growl in his throat.

'We'll ketch the varmints red-handed!' he gloated. 'I'll git a posse!'

'Wait!'

Mary Lester stood in the doorway determinedly and stopped Hoot Sampson.

'I don't want a posse after Rolf. I asked yuh to stop him gitting to the Monument Valley camp. Yuh've jest got to stop him, Clint. That's all I want! I don't want him caught robbin' the miners!'

Her voice was pleading desperately. Clint moistened dry lips. 'Mary —' he began.

'Will yuh jest stop Rolf from gittin' to the camp?' she persisted. 'That's all I want. I don't care what happens to Fogel. I jest want Rolf stopped. He's all I've got! He – he – he's my brother, Clint!'

There was a world of pleading in her tone. Clint swung undecidedly to Hoot Sampson.

'Yuh're the sheriff. What's it to be?'

'We're a-goin' to ketch the skunk red-handed shootin' into thet camp!' snapped Hoot. 'An' then we'll string him up!'

And Hoot Sampson stepped forward to push the girl to one side.

With surprising speed, Mary withdrew a small Derringer from within her shirt pocket. The sheriff halted at once, anger glinting in his eyes.

'Put thet away, gal!'

'Don't move – either of yuh!' Mary's voice was hard.

'What's the idee?' growled Hoot.

'You ain't goin' to ride after Rolf an' catch him red-handed shooting into the placer camp,' she said determinedly. 'You'll either do as I want, or you'll stay right here for as long as I kin hold yuh. That'll give Rolf plenty o' time to get away. There won't be no posse after him.'

Hoot breathed heavily, looked at Clint as if this was all his fault.

'Doggone it! Dogblastit! Women! Lissen hyar, gal, yuh can't keep us hyar! Yuh can't help thet no-good brother o' yourn!'

Clint tried to reason with her.

'Mary! This isn't any good. If Rolf is a-goin' to thet placer camp with the idee o' robbing, he'll have to take what's coming to him.'

'Promise you'll ride out and stop him afore he gits to the camp!' she pleaded.

Clint looked at the sheriff.

'What about it?' he asked quietly.

For a moment Hoot glared at them as if he contemplated rushing the Derringer and chancing the small bullet. Then he relented.

'All right. Let's hit leather. Anyhow, I figger a sheriff's job is to stop robbery as much as ketch the stinking polecats who do it!'

Mary replaced her Derringer in her shirt pocket with a sigh of relief.

'I'm a-goin' with you,' she announced. Clint caught her arm and said quietly:

'No, Mary. Monument Valley is desert country. It's a hard ride. An' there might be trouble.'

Her generous lips were firm. 'I'm a-goin', Clint.'

For the next few minutes, while Hoot led the horses out and filled water bottles, he tried to argue with her. But she would not change her mind.

'I'm a-goin', Clint. I want to be there.'

He gave up. She had a wiry roundup pony outside and had prepared for the ride. A canteen of water was tied to the saddle horn and a rifle was in the saddle holster.

They rode out as the sun climbed the sky like a blazing ball of fire. Hoot Sampson was grimly disgruntled, but he had kept his word and not called a posse. But he was chagrined at losing the chance to get Rolf Lester and any others red-handed.

As they cantered south along the banks of the river Rio Pecos, where grass grew green in spite of the scorching sun, Clint tried to gain some additional information from Mary.

'Have yuh any idee who this boss *hombre* kin be?'

'I don't know, Clint. I jest don't know.'

'But yuh overheard Rolf and Fogel talkin'?'

'Shore, I did, Clint. But all they said was, somethin' about meeting up with the boss. I didn't hear any name – and – and – I was rather frightened! I did hear about Monument Valley. Rolf was tellin' Fogel how much the placer workers were pickin' out o' the river. Then I saddled the pony and rode out.'

Clint – nodding grimly – stared over the land, through the shimmering heat waves.

'I've heard about the camp at Monument Valley. Nuthin' but a lot o' tents and shacks made o' hammered tin cans. Guess those fellers are panning gold, all right. Maybe a few hard *hombres* could raid the camp an' hold the miners at the point o' a rifle while some other jigger grabbed sacks o' dust. It's bin done afore.'

'They've got to be stopped!' she said tensely. 'Rolf might git killed! The miners might shoot back!'

'They shore will – iffen they git within reach o' a gun. Rolf is jest a hell-bent rannigan. Why'n heck can't he stick to ranching?'

Her lips, red, generous and made for smiling, were slightly bitter.

'He's jest wild and mean. He's bull-strong and reckless. He jest isn't civilized. And the ranch won't ever be a moneymaker. Scrub is growing in on the land all the time. We've got title to miles o' land but most of it is goin' desert. Why, I kin remember places on the spread which were lush with grass when the rains came, an' now those places are mostly sand an' cholla. The desert is creepin' in on the Circle Four.'

'Needs plenty o' hard work to keep the scrub out,' agreed Clint. 'Say, Mary, who owns title to the spread – yuh or Rolf?'

'We have a half share since Tad died,' she said quietly. 'That was part o' my father's Will.'

He nodded and rowelled his bay because Hoot was looking somewhat impatient. They rode at a full lope, following the twisting river. The Rio Pecos was entering rocky channels now and the country was semi-arid. Away in the distance, towering buttes rose from the plain with red, scoured walls. Here, at certain seasons, harsh winds full of sand and rain smoothed the red buttes like sandpaper on wood.

As they rode, they searched the horizon for sign of other riders. In the shimmering haze on the horizon, they often fancied they could see horses, but the distant objects always proved to be strangely-shaped cactus growths.

And then, like slowly moving dots, they caught sight of riders in the distance. The plain stretched ahead for miles, with semi-arid conditions. The land was a mixture of mesquite, shale and cholla. It was unwanted land. In the vastness of the plain, the towering buttes, with many miles between them, were like brooding guardians of the terrain.

The distant riders moved slowly along the red face of a vast butte. The horses seemed to be walking. As Clint squinted through the glare of the sun, the distant riders seemed to progress with the speed of insects.

Hoot Sampson's keen eyes had picked them out.

'Two o' them! Thet's the jiggers, I'll be allowed.'

'You kin stop them. Hurry!' cried Mary.

'How?' demanded Hoot. 'An' why the heck should I?'

'Yuh promised!'

Hoot growled

'Aw, all right! All right! But those *hombres* are blamed dangerous. An' they kin do us a good turn afore we cut them back like a herd o' mavericks.'

'What d'yuh mean, Hoot?' asked Clint.

'I mean I aim to let them jiggers ketch up with the feller they work fer!' said Hoot belligerently. 'I want to see this big boss who's behind all the rumpus!'

Clint was silent. He shot a glance at Mary. The horses cantered on all the time.

'Yuh're tryin' to trick me!' cried the girl.

'I ain't,' snapped Hoot stubbornly. 'But I'm shore anxious to set eyes on thet boss feller. I promise yuh them jiggers won't be raidin' the placer camp. We'll figger out some way to git across their trail an' stop 'em with a rifle. But only after I set eyes on thet boss rannigan.'

There was nothing Mary could do. It was futile to argue with the hard old sheriff. And they had yet to get ahead of the distant riders.

Clint left the situation at that. He had a hunch he would be playing a wise game if he said as little as possible. He wanted to gain Mary's sympathy.

Hoot took charge and led the way, riding across the plain to the left. They rode across hot, hard-baked sand with a red butte between them and the distant riders. Hoot cut a trail that led ahead of the two renegade riders, and owing to the position of the line of buttes, they could not be observed by Rolf Lester and Bert Fogel.

The river had curved, but anyone who wanted to hit Monument Valley with as little riding as possible, would not follow the twists of the river. The two men ahead were riding for some broken country up front, and the river swerved in a great loop to their right. Hoot knew this part of Texas like the palm of his hand. He was making a clever move. At the pace they were going, the trail would take them to the broken country before the other two men and they would be unobserved.

For half an hour the renegade riders were lost to view, but Hoot was confident of the direction of their trail. Soon the line of buttes merged into the broken land. Great heaps of volcanic boulders lay piled up for nearly a mile all round. It was as if nature, in some freak moment, had thrown the huge rocks together like a gigantic heap of rubble.

Clint, Mary and Hoot came round to this broken, rocky pileup miles from the spot where the sheriff estimated Rolf and Fogel would eventually hit.

They found cover and rode some distance through a cleft in the pileup. Then Hoot waved his hand and dismounted.

'I'm a-goin' to climb to a high spot in these rocks an' take a look-see fer those fellers,' he announced. 'Can't be fur from hyar now.'

The rugged old sheriff went up the sloping face of a huge slab of rock, digging his toes into the surface and scrambling on all fours. Glint grinned at Mary as they watched Hoot gain a vantage point, but the girl responded with only a faint smile. She was plainly worried.

Hoot planted himself at the top of the slab and spent some time staring into space. Then he slithered down again with a rasping of leather boots on rock.

'They met up wi' the boss!' he snapped. 'They're havin' a parley jest 'way off from this pileup an' there's three *hombres* now an' they got a spare hoss, too.'

'Guess we'll git along,' said Clint quietly.

'Yuh bet,' snapped Hoot. 'I want to git a look at thet boss jasper. Aw, if only we could ha' ketched 'em red-handed raidin' the placer camp!'

And Hoot turned in disgust to his horse.

They rode out of the cleft in single file, with the sheriff in the lead and Mary coming last. They skirted the pileup until they came to the outcrop that was the last bit of cover between them and the renegade riders.

Hoot halted the others.

'Clint, I want yuh to go over the top o' this heap a' goldarned rock and git around to the other side o' them fellers. I'll give yuh plenty o' time, but make it quick as yuh kin. Then when yuh sees me ride out with a rifle fixed on 'em, yuh walk out o' cover from the other side. We'll turn them fellers back to Laredo like a pack o' leery steers.'

Clint nodded. From Hoot's previous remarks he gathered that the three riders had stopped in the desert just off the rocky mass of boulders. Maybe they were resting the horses. Could hardly be any other reason for stopping. Anyway, Hoot and he could not skirt the outcrop any further without exposing themselves to the men. It would be better if they got them from two angles.

Clint dismounted, threw the reins to Mary and took his rifle from his saddle boot. He went up the rocky pileup, taking care not to go near the edge that sloped into the desert.

Moving swiftly, with sure feet, he made little noise. He encountered the thousand-spined cholla cactus and thickets of prickly pear, and had to make his way round the clumps. Twice he disturbed a basking rattler, but the yellow-backs slid away at his approach.

With keen eyes, he judged the spot to make for, and got to it after less than five minutes sure movement through the mass of rocks.

He waited. He could see the outcrop which hid Hoot Sampson. He gripped the rifle and dug in. Out on the red desert less than five hundred yards distant, the three riders were squatting on the sand. They were smoking, while the horses stood with hanging heads.

Clint fancied he could identify Rolf Lester even though the young rannigan had his back to him. Bert

Fogel, in his black shirt and hat, was easily placed. Clint narrowed his eyes. He was not sure of the third man. He just couldn't place him. There was nothing about his clothes or build that he could recognise. And the man was squatting with his back to the rocky pileup.

There were four horses grouped round the men. One was the spare animal. It was saddled.

'Got it all planned!' muttered Clint. 'I wonder who thet third feller is? I can understand old Hoot's feelings.'

Then, with silent drama, a horse nosed out of the distant outcrop. It was Hoot Sampson with his rifle levelled high over the animal's head. Behind him came Mary, leading Clint's bay.

Clint walked out at the same moment.

He went about ten yards before he heard Hoot bawl:

'Hoist 'em!'

'Don't reach!' rapped Clint from the other side.

The three men promptly stuck their hands above their shoulders. Rolf got slowly to his feet, his hands still high. He turned round to see Winchesters moving to him from two sides.

'Yuh danged nosy snakes!'

Hoot rode closer and stopped ten yards from the group. Clint came up from the opposite direction and halted.

'Yuh kin turn, *hombres*!' he snapped. 'But keep them hands high.'

Fogel turned heavily and flicked sardonic glances first at Hoot and then to Clint.

The third man turned and scowled first to the right and then to the left.

Clint stared at the man. He was a nondescript ruffian with owl-hoot written all over his unshaven face. Clint had never seen him before, but he knew instinctively that this man was not the person known as the boss.

The man was just another hired gunman.

Hoot Sampson's thoughts were identical with those held by his deputy. Sheer disgust moved over his face. His red moustache bristled.

'Who are yuh, feller?' he bawled, nodding at the man.

The man scowled back.

'What the hell's it to yuh? Why the gun-play?'

'Jest a lil joke from Sheriff Sampson!' drawled Fogel. 'He's got such a suspicious mind, he can't abide seein' three waddies ride out anyplace without gittin' trigger itch. What's on yore mind, Sheriff?'

'Yep. Yuh mind tellin' us what's goin' on?' shouted Rolf.

'Lissen, polecats, I know yuh figger to ride into the placer camp and grab dust. I shore did figger to fix eyes on thet boss o' yourn, but thar seems to be some mistake. Mebbe yuh ain't meetin' up with the boss this time.'

Rolf allowed a sneering grin to slide over his face.

'Yuh all tangled, Sheriff. We don't know what the blazes yuh're talkin' about!'

But his gaze fixed on Mary and the cold, inhuman gleam in his light blue eyes scared the girl.

Clint did not miss a thing.

'This ain't no Injun pow-pow!' bawled Hoot. 'Yuh're goin' to start ridin' fer Laredo now with me keepin' this goldarned rifle on yore backs, an' Clint hyar is goin' to ride to Monument Valley an' warn the miners about you skunks in case yuh figger to try some other time!'

Hoot had hardly got the angry words out when a rifle roared. He lurched in his saddle and dropped his rifle. He clutched at his side and blood spurted through his fingers. As the horse jibbed, he fell from the saddle with a sickening thud.

Clint had wheeled with the roar of the rifle in his ears.

A man was advancing from the pile of boulders, and his face was covered with a masking bandana.

The unknown carried a smoking rifle and it roared again, even as Clint desperately whipped his own Winchester up for a shot.

Instantly pain seared through Clint's head. A million jagged lights flashed before his eyes. There was one thought – the masked man was the boss!

And then thought died in a mile-deep pit of darkness.

He pitched forward as if dead.

# 7

# MASKED RAIDERS.

Mary Lester was stricken with the horror of it. She watched Clint pitch forward and although terror shuddered through her, she could not move a limb.

Hoot Sampson, too, lay sprawled on the desert sand. She could see a red patch on his shirt, and the sight of it sickened her. Dazedly, she turned her head to Rolf. A savage grin had spread over his face. He lumbered forward through the heavy sand and stared down at the motionless body of Clint Randall.

'Guess yuh fixed the galoot kinda permanent!' he guffawed to the approaching masked man.

The unknown turned his head and pointed the rifle at Mary.

'Maybe I should deal with her.'

Rolf Lester's twisted smile faded very slowly. A bleak expression changed the colour of his eyes.

'She's my sister!'

'She might be dangerous.'

'Yuh got a mask, ain't yuh?' snapped Rolf.

Mary sat in the saddle numb with horror. Too late she remembered the Derringer she carried. If she tried to get it the stranger would shoot her. She knew that.

'I had to git you *hombres* out of a bad spot!' sneered the boss. 'A good thing these damned fools didn't figger yuh were waitin' for me to ride up. Maybe it was lucky for you I was kinda late.'

Rolf swung to his sister and his smooth young face was set savagely.

'Yuh must ha' put these gents on to our trail!'

'That makes her dangerous, as I said,' commented the masked boss.

Rolf swung back again and snapped at him:

'But yuh kin quit worrying about her. I'll take her in hand. She won't give no trouble. An' she can't split on yuh. She don't know yuh from Adam!'

'All right,' grated the man. 'Git to yore hosses. We're ridin' to the placer camp. Those miners ha' got more dust out thet river than they ever had afore. An' we are a-goin' to git it.'

'Thet's the job!' guffawed Fogel.

Rolf grinned and stamped over to his cayuse. The others grabbed at reins and leaped to leather.

Shock drained out of Mary and she jumped from her horse and ran over to Clint.

It came as a terrible blow to her to realize how much she really cared for this tall, slow-speaking westerner.

She reached him and saw the horrible red blood welling from the side of his head. Her breath choked her. She reached out blindly to turn him round when Rolf's hand gripped her and jerked the girl to her feet.

'Git on yore hoss.'

'You – you – you've helped to kill him!'

'Fergit it! I didn't shoot him anyway. The boss did. Git on yore hoss. We're ridin' fer Monument Valley, an' yuh'll have to come along with us. Jest shut up and yuh'll be safe.'

She tried to struggle. He held her and found the Derringer. He took it from the pocket and pushed it into his belt.

Then he picked her up and carried her to her horse and pushed her into the saddle. She sat for a moment helpless.

There was nothing she could do. Clint was dead. Hoot was either dead or dying, his blood draining into the desert sand.

Rolf jigged his big horse to hers. He grabbed at the bridle and led the horse over to the others.

'All right! Let's git alawng!' snapped the boss.

The four men formed round the girl's horse. Steel rowels were fed to sweating flanks and the horses sprang into a full lope. As they headed across the desert, they left only a trail of dust to mark their path.

Two riderless horses nosed in the scrub for bits of grass. On the desert floor two men sprawled.

Mary Lester felt a terrible sense of unnameable horror and a pitiful realization of her helplessness. She saw clearly that nothing could turn her brother from the path along which his reckless nature had taken him. Lawlessness was in his blood. She had tried to stop something beyond her capacity when she had tried to keep him straight.

The riders thundered over the arid land and the buttes which gave Monument Valley its name became clearer in the heat haze. The buttes were red and fantastically shaped. Erosion by wind and rain had carved many marvellous contours in the sides of the towering masses of rocks. The river wound in close to the buttes in one of its erratic sweeps.

There was one red butte which hugged the river, and the riders came close to the towering walls and slowed to a walk. After another hundred yards, the masked boss halted the party.

There, in a flat plain of shale and sand which bounded the slow river, was the placer camp. The tents and shacks were high above the river bank. The place was a sorry, ramshackle dump. It was amazing to think that the men who stood kneedeep in the river were winning gold in quantities sufficient to buy them good homes when they could get away from the place.

The placer claims were a hive of industry. All along the river bed men worked at building small dams, panning the silt and water. The Rio Pecos brought down gold in minute chips whenever there were floods, and the gold settled into the silt when the river was sluggish. This bend of the river was rich in gold. The contours of the rivers had caused silt to pile up and in the silt was gold for the panning.

'Nice hard workers!' drawled the masked boss. 'All right! Don't make a helluva din! We ride down an' spread out along the river an' make these panners reach fer the sky. They ain't got no guns while they're workin' in that river. Everything's nice and stacked in them shacks – includin' the gold. You, Clip!'

'Yep?' inquired the fourth rannigan, the typical border ruffian.

'Yore job is to git among those shacks and git the

dust while we keep them blamed miners reachin'.
Work as fast as yuh kin. This ain't no party.'

The four hell-bent renegades knew the miners
were hard men who would chance death if they
figured they could beat those who attempted to rob
them. But ruthlessness was the very nature of Rolf
Lester and Bert Fogel. Killing meant nothing to
them; it was merely a way of living.

The horses picked a way slowly along the ridge
that led along the river bank. The boss went ahead to
the furthest point, his hat well down, his chin sunk
on his chest. Fogel and Rolf strung out behind him
and the man called Clip sat his horse waiting the
signal.

The renegades just ignored Mary. She was a
woman and they apparently felt contemptuous of her
ability to do anything to stop their plans.

Hardly seconds elapsed before the boss rode his
horse over the slope and dawn to the river. Rolf and
Fogel followed, spaced at hundred yard distances.
Their appearance was swift as magic to the busy
placer miners. One or two chanced to look up and
saw menacing rifles pointing at them.

'Hoist 'em!' roared the masked boss, and Rolf and
Fogel added their commands simultaneously.

It was a strange sight. All along the river miners
straightened weary backs and stared at the three
horsemen and the rifles. For a distance of over three
hundred yards every miner was covered by the slowly
moving rifles. Only a few miners had Colts stuck in
their belts. Working in water was no place to carry a
gun. And they dared not use them against men with
rifles.

The element of surprise was with the robbers. They sat motionless and wary, high on their horses. Rolf and Fogel had pulled bandanas up over their mouths. Hats were well down.

Only glinting, savagely amused, eyes stared over the scene and did not miss a thing.

The man named Clip was busy going through the shacks. First he kicked the door in and entered with Colt in hand. Luck was with him. All the placer miners were down at the river. Clip grabbed at sacks of dust. They were usually hidden behind bedrolls or stowed away in boxes. In one or two shacks Clip could not find any dust. Either the miner had sold the gold or had buried it. Swearing filthily, Clip lurched to the next stop. This was a crude, canvas tent, man-high.

Clip pushed in and saw the haggard man lying on the floor covered with dirty blankets. He was apparently ill.

The miner raised a gun with hands that shook.

Clip's shooting iron roared first and the slug flattened against bone, tearing a hole in the miner's head.

Clip kicked round the tent, but again there was no gold to be found. He stamped out of the tent, bawled assurance to his companions and then plunged into the next tin-can shack.

He carried a canvas poke. Within ten minutes, the poke was getting full and heavy. It did not need many small sacks of dust to weigh down a man. But Clip went on, impelled by greed and the thought that his share would be greater if he grabbed as much gold as possible.

Down at the river the miners were getting restless. One or two, inwardly mad with rage, had crept out of the silt inch by inch.

One man had a gun stuck into his belt. He figured be could use it on the nearest masked rider – if he could only get a few yards nearer. At the moment the range was too much for reliable shooting.

Rolf, Fogel and the unknown boss had noted the almost imperceptible movement of some of the miners. But they figured the men were not dangerous as yet.

All at once, rage consumed the miner with the gun in his belt. He leaped forward, crouching and weaving. The gun was in his fist. It spat lead at the masked boss, but at extreme range the slugs went wide. The man's weaving and ducking spoilt his own aim.

The boss's rifle spoke. It belched red and the miner threw up his arms and his body contorted. He crashed to the shale and lay still.

All at once, Clip gave his shrill whistle. It was a signal that he had cleaned up. He was staggering back to the two horses.

The three masked riders jigged the horses crabwise up the sloping river bank. Not for a second did the Winchesters cease to point menacingly at the glowering miners.

Clip worked fast, tying the poke to the saddle of the spare horse. He was gloating. Even split four ways – with a bonus for the boss – there was plenty of gold in the poke. Enough to give a *hombre* a month of drinking and gambling in some lawless border town – and all for a day's work! The plan had been the idea of the boss. He was a good *hombre* to work for!

The three riders withdrew to the ridge of the river bank. The boss threw a quick glance at Clip. He had finished fastening the heavy poke of stolen gold bags to the spare horse, and was in the saddle of his own horse.

'Feed 'em steel!' shouted the boss. It was the signal for the getaway.

Four riders and the laden spare horse thundered away from the river and tore round the red butte at a full lope. Dust rose to mark their trail.

It was then Rolf realised Mary had gone. Riding low in the saddle, he turned this way and that and stared over the land, but he could not see the girl.

He cursed and fed more steel to his galloping mount.

Back at the placer camp the miners scrambled for horses and rifles. But few of the horses were saddled, and time was wasted. Two miners rode out ahead of the others but even they were badly behind time.

The miners rode out in a straggling line a good way behind the robbers. They saw the renegades urging their big horses away into the distance. Ten minutes later the broken country swallowed the bandits and the trail was lost. The boss planned well.

Mary Lester had turned her pony even before the raid had started. There was nothing she could do to prevent the raid. She had only one idea. She was obsessed with the urge to ride back to where Hoot Sampson and Clint lay. She just had to go back. There was no logic in it. She knew as well as anyone that she could not help a dead man. But she had had to return to the spot where the men sprawled so dreadfully in the desert. She was not sure that Hoot

Sampson was dead. But as sure as there was heaven and earth, he would die out there without attention.

She urged the pony on, taking a direct course through the red buttes of Monument Valley. She had a good sense of direction and had ridden over this arid land before in happier, better times. Whenever she thought of Rolf back at the placer camp, a grim, hard feeling rose under her heart.

If he got himself killed, he would have only himself to blame! Perhaps – perhaps – it would be better if he was dead! It would be nothing more than justice. Rolf had killed before.

Appalled and confused at her thoughts, she urged the pony on and on as if the swiftness of her ride would help her tormented mind.

She rode through brush and thorn, silvery cholla and grotesque Joshua trees, galloping the pony out of the red butte country and heading across the arid plain. Away on her right was the gigantic pileup of volcanic boulders which stretched for more than a mile and was the home of cholla, prickly pear and rattlers. She did not know that four human rattlers would shortly make for the pileup and shake off the pursuing miners!

She headed the pony over the plain towards the pileup. As it came nearer she veered again and went round the outskirts of the volcanic heap of rock to the spot where she knew Hoot and Clint had been shot.

She wondered about the boss. She had a slight suspicion as to his identity, but was not sure.

She wished she had grabbed at his masking bandana. Perhaps – perhaps – if she could hand the boss over to justice, Rolf might reform.

Deep in her heart she knew that was utterly impossible now. Rolf was lawless. If he made mistakes and had to run for it, he would be a wanted man. His features would go up on Wanted posters outside sheriffs' offices. He would have to take to the owl-hoot trail.

Again she flung the grim thoughts from her. The pony galloped on, wide-eyed and mane flying. They skirted the large rocky island in the desert – and then, suddenly it seemed, she came upon the two shot men and their horses.

She saw Clint sitting up and amazement and relief flooded through her. He was attending to Hoot Sampson. He had propped the sheriff against a rock. The horses stood nearby, docilely.

She leaped from her horse and ran to him. Her soft, bronzed features showed her love for him. Her compassionate blue eyes saw the ugly red wound along the side of his head, and she knew it was a crease. The bullet had seared along the side of his head, stunning him. Another half-inch and he would have died instantly.

With the sheer wonder and relief of it making her tremble, she flung her arms round him.

'Oh, Clint, yuh're all right! Yuh're alive! Oh, God, I'm so glad!' She swung to Hoot. 'Is he – alive?' she breathed.

'He's jest alive!' he said grimly. 'Gawd knows if he'll stay thet way.'

'Is he badly wounded?'

'Yep. The bullet went through his side and came out again. Old Hoot has kinda got two holes in him!'

It was a grim jest, but the way of men in the west. The sheriff of Laredo was unconscious still.

'Lost a lot o' blood,' said Clint, thin-lipped. 'Yuh kin see it in the sand.'

She looked and was sickened by the red patch nearby. She looked up as something wheeled across the glaring blue sky.

'Buzzards!' said Clint.

'Yuh've got to git to the Doc!' she insisted.

He stood up and swayed. He planted his feet apart and tried to steady his world. Everything was a sickening swirl.

'Fifteen miles o' ridin',' he muttered. 'But we'll have to make it. We've jest got to git Hoot to Doc Hawton. He's the only medico fer miles.'

Clint had used two bandanas to provide a tight bandage round Hoot's middle. That had helped to stem the bleeding. They raised the sheriff to the saddle of Clint's bay.

'I'll ha' to ride with him,' said Clint. 'The old cuss would fall off by himself. Reckon the bay kin take double.'

He mounted slowly, without his usual lithe swing. He hunkered down on the leather. Mary got to her saddle and rode stirrup to stirrup with him. They took the other horse in lead.

'What happened?' asked Clint as they jogged off.

'They made me go with them. They raided the placer camp so far as I know. I jest rode away. They never gave a thought to me.'

'Wonder iffen them hellions got shot!' muttered Clint hopefully.

'I don't know,' she said dully. 'I jest don't know –

and I don't care!' she ended fiercely.

'Mary,' he began quietly, 'there just ain't nuthin' anyone kin do for Rolf. He's jest plumb hell-bent. I want to know this – yuh don't hate me fer goin' after him, do yuh?'

She shook her head.

'Yuh've got a job to do. I've bin a fool, Clint. When will it all be over?'

He was silent. The horses plodded on, stirrup to stirrup, and then he said harshly:

'It'll all be over when Rolf is dead an' thet boss rannigan is swinging from a cottonwood!'

She sank her head slowly to her chin and rode on in silence. Then she raised her head, and he saw the tears, the tremble of her lips.

'I won't do anythin' to stop yuh, Clint,' she said.

And then she stared proudly ahead, her head high. He loved her then and was inarticulate. He could think of nothing to say, and there was nothing he could do for he was still groggy with the wound. They rode on, and he watched her. She looked fine and lovely. It was incredible to imagine she had a wild brother like Rolf. Tad Lester was dead, and he had killed him. But time was healing that sorrow. She was forgetting it.

His head throbbed dully and it was a trouble to think. He had to keep Hoot upright in the saddle and the sheriff was a heavy man. From time to time he rolled like a sack of potatoes, and Clint held his weight with one arm. Heat shimmered down from the red orb high in the brilliant blue sky. There was not the slightest sign of a wispy white cloud. The arid sand and shale glared back and, with the pain in his head, sickened him. But fifteen miles was not too much, he figured. All he had to do was stick in the leather and the cayuse would hit town.

He was really worried about Hoot Sampson. Although the old-timer was not dead, he had lost a lot of blood and the bullet might have caused internal injuries. Only a doctor could tell and the doc was in Laredo.

The boss had shot quickly and assumed too much. Maybe he was a clever *hombre*, but he was liable to make mistakes.

'Did yuh git a chance to study thet boss rannigan?' he asked the girl.

'I watched him, Clint.'

'D'yuh know the gent? I didn't set eyes on him long afore he creased me.'

She hesitated.

'I think he was Dave Lansing.'

'D'yuh see his face?'

'No. I can't be shore. There was jest something about the way he sat his hoss. I don't know, Clint. Maybe I'm wrong.'

'It's a tip,' he muttered. 'Jest like Hoot sez – we've got to git them *hombres* red-handed.'

The horses had hardly plodded on more than four miles towards Laredo when a rising cloud of dust on the horizon behind them denoted riders. Mary had turned and seen the dust and brought it to Clint's attention.

'Hoof dust,' he said. 'Riders a-comin' this way.'

It was apparent the riders had spotted them, for the black shapes on the yellow land grew larger. Men were rowelling galloping horses. Soon the riders thundered across the waste and reined in alongside Clint and Mary.

They saw the deputy badge on Clint's shirt and put guns back in holsters and saddle boots.

'Yuh're miners,' said Clint with an expert glance at their mud-spattered pants and vests. 'Yuh lookin' fer those thievin' *hombres*?'

'Yep. What ye know about them, Deputy?' asked a large, gaunt Irishman.

'The sheriff an' me tried to stop them busting in on yuh. The sheriff got gunned. I've got to git him back to Laredo.'

The Irishman stared shrewdly and noted the red wound along Clint's head where his hat was cocked up to prevent chafing the wound.

'Sure, and ye bin shot yoreself.' The Irish miner turned to one of his pals. 'Joe, ye got a big strong cayuse. By the saints, ye kin help to git the sheriff in to Laredo. Take the sheriff on yore hoss, Teller.'

Clint was glad of the help. Hoot Sampson was transferred to the big black roan which Joe rode.

'Wal, looks like them skunks ha' lost us off!' growled the gaunt Irishman. 'But iffen we git 'em, we'll string 'em up, Deputy.'

'Yuh ought to bring 'em in for a trial,' said Clint quietly.

'Trial, be danged!' roared the miner. 'There ain't many trees down by the river, but by holy heck we'll shore find one – iffen we kin cut sign o' them robbers. Ha' ye any idee who they may be, Deputy?'

Clint took a deep breath. He did not look at Mary.

'One feller is called Bert Fogel and he manages he Last Chance saloon at Laredo.'

'Do he now? Guess I'll remember thet name. How about the other jaspers?'

'One o' them is a feller called Rolf Lester,' gritted Clint. 'The other galoots we ain't shore about.'

'Who is this Rolf Lester?'

Clint straightened up and answered.

'He half-owns the Circle Four close by Laredo – six miles west.'

'Thanks, Deputy. We'll remember them names. Thet placer feller died. One o' them robbers kilt him. Thet makes 'em murderers – all on 'em!'

'They've killed afore thet!' said Clint harshly.

'Thet so? Wal, we fellers aim to git some satisfaction. We'll git 'em.'

The miners, with the exception of a man called Joe O'Rourke, turned their horses and veered across the arid land again. They were returning to the broken terrain where they had lost the trail.

Joe O'Rourke intended to ride in with Sheriff Hoot Sampson. Joe had a respect for the law.

Clint rode close to Mary, and he reached out and took her hand.

'Yuh know what this means,' he said. 'Rolf and Fogel won't dare show up in Laredo agin. With Hoot an' me alive, we could convince a judge and jury thet those rannigans raided the placer camp and killed a man. They won't risk it. They're on the run now, Mary!'

# 8

# DEATH KNIFE

Mary Lester nodded dumbly at the words, and flashed a glance at Joe O'Rourke but the miner was intent upon riding carefully with his burden.

She knew Clint had summarised the situation clearly. As soon as Rolf knew that Hoot Sampson and Clint Randall were still alive – and the word would soon come to the boss – he would know his reckless living had got him into a precarious position. It would not really worry him, so long as he evaded capture. He hated being tied to the ranch, and there were hideouts in Pueblo which had the advantage of being over the border and out of reach of Texas lawmen. The same state of affairs would hit Fogel the same way.

They were outlaws!

Clint was too tired for conjecture. When they rode into Laredo some hours later the sun was swinging down from its place overhead. Hoot Sampson was put to rest in his bed and Doc Hawton summoned. Mary Lester stayed by Clint. Doc Hawton did his best for the deputy, and soon a nice white bandage graced

Clint's head. He could hardly get his hat on.

'Goldarn it!' he growled. 'How long have I got to wear this?'

'Till thet wound dries!' snapped Doc Hawton.

The medico could drop his pedantic speech whenever it suited him!

'Hows about Hoot? He's a-goin' to be all right, ain't he?'

'He'll live,' said the doctor grimly, 'but he won't be riding horses for some weeks. He's lost a lot of blood, and he'll have to rest.'

'Wal, yuh ain't got to probe fer the bullet!' grinned Clint, in relief.

The news went round the town pretty quickly, and while there were necessarily a few desperadoes who regretted that the sheriff and his deputy had not passed out in the desert, the bulk of the population resented the shooting of their appointed lawmen. The news passed around that Rolf Lester and Bert Fogel, along with a man named Clip and another unknown, were responsible for the shooting and the raid on the distant placer camp.

Mary Lester insisted upon riding back to her ranch alone. Regretfully, Clint watched her go. There were so many things he wanted to ask her, and yet he knew this was still the wrong time.

He insisted on taking some action, despite Doc Hawton's warning that he would be asking for a mighty sick head if he did not rest. Clint grinned, figured he had had sick heads before, and went out into the dusty street.

He called at the Last Chance. Two bartenders were serving though it was a slack period of the day. Of

Fogel there was no sign. Clint hadn't thought there would be.

He went on to Malcolm Starn's freight-line office. A wagon was drawn up outside and packers were working. Clint walked in and found Starn bending over a ledger. One arm was still bandaged.

'How's the arm today?' rapped Clint.

Starn looked up. A thin smile flitted across his tight features. 'Fair enough, Randall.'

Clint waited until the packer had left the office.

'Lissen, Mister Starn, Bert Fogel has bin gun-totin' again. Thet's the only job he kin really do. How come yuh hired him fer the Last Chance?'

'I figured I told yuh once,' said Starn slowly. 'I wanted a strong *hombre* for thet saloon.'

'Thet jigger does as he likes. He ain't never in the durned saloon. Yuh ain't tellin' me the truth, Mister Starn. Let me tell yuh what's happened today.'

Clint gave the freight-line owner the events in a few clipped sentences.

'Ha' yuh bin here all day, Starn?' rapped Clint.

'As a matter o' fact, I have. I've had a kinda hard day loading the freight wagons. I've got to check things personally.'

'Kin yuh prove it?'

'Shore,' said Starn quietly.

He waited until the packer came in. The man was a little wizened fellow and an ex-puncher if his bandy legs were any guide.

'Can yuh tell the deputy where I've bin all day, Bill?' exclaimed Starn, and he detained the little man with one hand. Bill wrinkled his forehead in surprise.

'Bin? Why, yuh bin hyar – ain't yuh? We bin loadin' ain't we?'

'All day?' questioned Clint.

'Yep. All the danged day long!'

Clint smiled and nodded. A minute later when another man came through the office on his way to a store room, Clint stopped him.

'Kin yuh tell me something, pardner? Has Mister Starn bin working all the day with yuh?'

The man frowned as he thought, and then nodded.

'Shore. We bin at it all the blamed day. Time we took a durned spell. Why the heck yuh ask, Deputy?'

'Fergit it,' said Clint.

When the man had gone, he nodded curtly at Starn.

'All right. Yuh're cleared, Starn. Yuh ain't the boss who hires Rolf Lester an' Fogel an' other blasted rannigans.'

'Did yuh figure I was?'

'Not exactly. But yuh acted blamed queer. Suppose yuh spill it how yuh got thet wrist shot the same night the train was about to be derailed?'

Starn hesitated; then:

'I was down at the railroad when the posse shot up the bandits.'

'Yuh was? What the heck for?'

'I wanted to kill the boss.'

Clint narrowed his eyes.

'Who is the boss an' how come yuh figger to kill him?'

Malcolm Starn was a smallish man. He drew himself up stiffly and replied.

'The boss is Dave Lansing. I've been wantin' to kill

him for a long time. Fogel gave me a hint that some-thing was brewin' thet night an' I kept tag on Lansing. I figured I might be able to kill him during the raid on the train when lead would be kinda flying around. The posse started shootin' instead. I was in thet defile. I couldn't git a bead on Lansing, and then I got hit by a bullet. Gawd knows who shot at me. I had to ride back.'

'Why the blazes did yuh want to kill Lansing?'

'Lansing knew me long ago afore either o' us ever hit Laredo,' said Malcolm Starn bitterly. 'I'm a wanted man, Randall. There's a sheriff in Tucson who wants me for a killing. It's a lawng story, but I killed a feller in self-defence. I wasn't goin' to be given a chance to prove self-defence, so I lit out. I've bin in Laredo years an' never packed a gun. I've built up a business, got money in the bank and own prop-erty, includin' the Last Chance. Lansing kinda black-mailed me into hiring Fogel. I've bin paying thet feller money long enough. I guess Lansing thought Fogel could figger out some dandy alibis if he was fixed up in the saloon. An' he could meet rannigans and talk without suspicion. Kinda handy setup. Thet's why I had to hire Fogel.'

'Kin yuh tell me why yuh rode to Pueblo to meet up with Seth Mundy, Rolf Lester an' Fogel?'

'Wal, I jest guessed Fogel would make for Pueblo. Soon as I heard there'd bin a robbery at the gold company, I knew thet skunk would be behind it, an' I figured they'd make for Pueblo. It was jest a guess that came off.'

'What did yuh reckon to do?' asked Clint curi-ously. Starn's bitter eyes stared out of the office window.

'I thought I'd git a gun on thet feller when he was out over the border. Killin' ain't nothin' in Pueblo. They've got no sheriff or marshal. 'But the idee didn't git a chance.'

'Wal, Fogel ain't comin' back to Laredo,' said Clint. 'An' maybe it won't be long afore we hogtie Lansing. We'll call it a day, Mister Starn, an' quit worryin' about thet sheriff up in Tucson. We never got no Wanted bill about yuh in the Laredo office. Could be yuh ain't wanted no more.'

He left the freight-line owner and mentally cancelled him from his thoughts. Malcolm Starn was certainly not the boss. The dying miner whom Clint had found in the sandstorm had been right, but Fogel had linked up with Dave Lansing and not Starn.

The suspicions against Lansing were building up, but so far there was not much proof. Even if Starn intended to accuse Lansing of blackmail, proof would have to be got. Documentary proof was needed, and the probability was that there was not any. No one could prove that Dave Lansing had ridden with the holdup men who exchanged lead with the posse, and Mary could not be sure that Lansing had been the leader in the placer camp raid. Rolf Lester and Bert Fogel probably knew the extent of Dave Lansing's crookedness, but those gun-toters were all in the swim together.

As Clint walked steadily down the dusty main street, passing the rattling buckboards, stray riders, cowboys, women in bonnets and shawls, ranchers and gamblers, he drew near to the Bonanza saloon. On the impulse he walked through the batwing doors. The interior was dim in comparison to the brightness of the late afternoon sun. He walked to the counter, found a bartender waiting expectantly with a bottle. Clint stared around, stopped when he saw Dave Lansing leaning against the counter, on the customer's side of the bar. Lansing was smiling, watching him, unperturbed.

'Howdy, Deputy!'

Clint took his drink, paid for it and swallowed it at once. He felt he needed it. His head still felt numb on one side. He came closer to Lansing.

'Jest got back?'

'As a matter o' fact, shore, Deputy. Bin over to Pueblo.'

'Yuh don't say. Shore it weren't Monument Valley?'

Dave Lansing smoothed his black suit. It was spotless. 'Nope. I said Pueblo, Deputy. Bin seeing pals. They'll tell yuh, if yuh interested. What's this about Monument Valley?'

'Figger yuh ought to know all about Monument Valley – it's all over town!' rapped the deputy.

There was nothing to get out of Dave Lansing, but the call had served the purpose of riling the man. It was Clint's opinion that a riled man would make a move sooner or later that might prove disastrous for him.

Clint had an idea there were buyers in Pueblo who would take gold at bargain prices and no questions asked. Had the four raiders got to the Mexican town?

He determined to find out.

He knew the Mexican town was not in his jurisdiction and he could not lawfully arrest a man there. But there were times when Clint was willing to take matters into his own hands. He wanted to take a look at Pueblo that night. He knew he could not take a posse over to search for Rolf or Fogel or the man named Clip. But he could ride over himself and see what was cooking, if anything.

He was not fool enough to wear himself to a thin wedge. He rested for an hour. His head felt better after that. He went to the eat-house and tucked some red beef away, then went up to see Hoot and found the sheriff conscious now.

Doc Hawton was still around.

'We've only got one sheriff,' said the medico man. 'And the ruffians who are, at this moment, busy shooting and cutting each other can patch each other up. I am in attendance upon Sheriff Sampson.'

'Good fer yuh,' retorted Clint. 'How d'yuh feel, oldtimer?'

In response, Hoot mustered a low growl.

'I aim to git the rannigan who shot me ribs! I ain't fergettin' anything!'

'Maybe I'll git him first,' said Clint. 'Yuh'll be hog-tied in this bed for a week or two. I aim to beat yuh to gettin' a hogleg on them hellions.'

He did not say anything of his plans, but went to the livery and got a fresh horse. The bay had had enough riding for one day, and the animals were there for use.

'Git plumb lazy iffen yuh don't git exercise, hoss!' muttered Clint as he tightened the cinch on the animal.

Ten minutes later he rode out with a quick tattoo of hoofs and headed over the land towards Pueblo.

The yellowed grass was left behind and the arid

land went under the horse's hoofs. Sage tainted the night air. Dust and sage, that was the aroma of the desert land. Moonlight glinted silvery on the cholla spines. Skeleton-like occotillo loomed up strangely in the night.

After a fast ride he entered the ramshackle town. He saw the yellow light spilling across the road, coming from the cantinas. Hoarse laughter provided the noise to a background of tinkling guitars. The *vaqueros* were making merry with drink and frowsy *senoritas.*

He hitched the horse to a cantina tie-rail where it would not be conspicuous among some others. He mounted the boardwalk and decided to stand in the shadow for some time. He made a brown paper cigarette and lit it with a thick sulphur match. Puffing luxuriously at the black tobacco he wondered if he was not wasting his time. Maybe he should have gone to bed!

But there was just that chance that Rolf, Fogel and the man named Clip were still in Pueblo. They would not be anywhere else. Pueblo, situated over the border, and with its sheer lack of law, was the best possible place.

He watched keenly as a few *vaqueros* rode in through the straggling main stem. They were all Mexicans in steeple-shaped hats and shapeless tilmas. There were curses and greetings in Spanish, snatches of wild song. As one batch trooped into the cantina, Clint walked through the batwing doors behind them.

Inside the place a motley crowd of men leaned against the pine counter and stood in groups. There were tables at which breeds gambled with savage intensity. A wrong word or movement, and the gamblers would be at each other's throats. The Mexicans liked the knife. A few half-breeds carried heavy Colts in fancy holsters.

A *senorita*, with a white blouse that threatened to slip further down white shoulders, sang from a table top, and a velvet-jacketed *vaquero* strummed a guitar as accompanist.

So much noise was going on that no one took any notice of Clint. No one even noticed his deputy badge.

But Clint had the faculty of being able to weigh up a crowded place in seconds.

He saw the man named Clip edge away from the bar at the other end of the room as if he had suddenly discovered there was small-pox around!

Clint smiled thinly at the scowl that erased the drunken grin from the man's face.

He watched the *hombre* slip to a side door, only stopping to down his drink.

It was the stop that gave Clint time to push through the crowd of Mexicans, half-breeds and border-type whites.

He went through the door in double-quick time, and found himself in a dark and smelly alley behind the cantina. There was nothing but alkali dust and the vague outline of shacks ahead.

He cursed, feeling that he had let the man slip.

He remembered the *hombre* when he and Hoot had held him up with rifles - remembered the scowl that characterised his face. Mary Lester had told him the man was called Clip. He knew nothing else about him. But this was the rannigan that had helped Fogel and Rolf raid the placer camp.

To his right a dark patch moved.

Clint was as silent as an Indian. He figured dark patches should not move without reason. There was just the slightest suspicion of someone lurking in the deep shadow of the adjacent store building.

Clint Randall tensed his muscles and shot across the intervening gap like an arrow. Even in the seconds that occupied his rush, a shot rang out.

Clint saw the belching red flame and felt the rush of the slug past his face. Another near one!

He could have scooped his Colts out and blasted the fellow into the next world there and then, but he had another idea. He gave no chance for a second shot. The man's gun had roared once and missed. Then Clint was on him.

He gripped the man by the wrist and forced the gun upwards. Once more the trigger squeezed and flame spat skywards. Then a savage jerk by Clint nearly broke the man's wrist and the gun dropped to the ground.

With his other hand, Clint Randall pinned the man's shoulders against the wall. The man tried to hack out with his boots. Clint brought his hand away from the fellow's wrist and rammed it into his stubbly chin. He did it three times and brought panting gasps out of the rannigan.

'Lissen, feller, yuh're the jigger who raided the placer camp. Yuh an' Rolf and Fogel. Where are those coyotes right now?'

'Yuh kin go to hell! I don't know where they are. Yuh're in Mexico, skunk!'

'I reckon yuh do know where them gents are hidin'!' rapped Clint. 'An' I aim to make yuh tell.'

He slammed his fist repeatedly into the man's mouth. He felt his knuckles grate against teeth, and wet blood slime his fist and he was grim. The man began to groan and his struggles slackened.

Clint eased off and breathed hard.

'All right, feller, spill it. Where do I find yore ornery pals?'

'Rolf – and – Fogel are – at – the Circle Four right now!' The words snarled at him between great gulps for air.

Clint released him. He did not realize he was making a mistake.

'Thet's fine,' snapped the deputy. 'Them gents are right in Texas territory an' they're wanted men. Fine.'

Without warning, a second or two after Clint's grasp came away, the man doubled up sharply. He seemed to bend down and ram his fingers into his high riding boots.

Clint saw the gleam of steel jerking up with a savage, hacking movement.

The man had withdrawn a long-bladed knife from his boot. It was a Mexican trick, probably learned in the lawless border town.

The deputy jerked his body back as the knife swung up in a movement that should have disembowelled him. The blade even ripped up his shirt cutting it like paper. As the man's arm continued up in its momentum, Clint moved in closer again and fastened his right hand on the man's wrist. The knife was forced above the rannigan's head. Relentlessly,

Clint pushed the man's arm back and back until both men were panting with the strain. Suddenly the man named Clip cried hoarsely as his arm seemed to reach breaking point. The knife fell from his nerveless grasp. It fell to the ground unnoticed by the combatants.

Clint stepped back, angry, grim and relentless. This man was a murderer and without any worthwhile characteristics. Clint's fists shot out. He planted two – a right and left that snapped the man's head up and back in agony. The rannigan stumbled back, boots digging in the dust. He fell backwards under the impact of the driving blows and lay still, staring at the wan moon.

Clint just stood and breathed deeply. Then, feeling that the rannigan had rested in the dust long enough, he bent down and hauled the man to his feet.

It was then Clint saw the knife rammed at an acute angle into the man's back. He stared into the rannigan's face. The man was dead.

He had fallen on his own knife.

Clint looked down at the ground, puzzled. It needed only a second's thought to see how the man had died.

A border of white boulders ran along the base of the store building. Apparently the knife had fallen into a crevice between the small boulders. Having a long blade, the knife had projected sufficiently to kill the renegade as he fell on it. Clint laid the body down grimly.

'I reckon I'll let the burial jiggers hyar take yuh to the Pueblo boothill!' he muttered. 'Me – I'm on my way!'

He moved stiffly round to the front of the cantina and unhitched his horse. The hubbub still arose from the drinking palace. Apparently the two shots in the night meant nothing.

Clint grinned thinly.

'Wal, I got out o' thet with a whole skin. Thet jigger jest got what was due to a doggone owl-hoot!'

He knew exactly what he intended to do.

He had not to forget he was deputy sheriff of Laredo and as such could not play a lone game. If Rolf Lester had taken Fogel to the Circle Four under the impression he could fool around safely, Clint knew it was his duty to get a posse and go after the men. Ridding a town of lawless men was a hard, grim job. The quicker it was over the better. And a posse was sure to get the men where one man might fail.

He did not spare the horse as he thundered back towards Laredo. He knew he could get a fresh mount when he rode out to the Circle Four with the posse.

The arid land flew under the animal's drumming hoofs. He had a sure-footed cayuse, for it avoided holes and loose shale admirably although the wan moonlight was not too good.

The horse moved swiftly from the desert land and into the sun-browned grass-lands near Laredo. He hit the trail and urged the horse on. He rode right through Laredo with a rapid tattoo of hoofs, threw himself off at the sheriff's office and led the horse into the livery, rousing the wrangler sleeping at the back in his cabin. The oldster promised to have a fresh horse saddled when Clint returned.

Clint went down to the Bonanza saloon, knowing that Fogel would not be there. He found three rough and ready cowboys who he knew. They nodded at his request. Quietly they left the saloon, two of them with small flasks of whisky stuffed in the pockets of their flapping vests! They intended to have their night's drink at any cost!

There was a quieter saloon nearby, much frequented by the better class of responsible rancher. Clint got two possemen without any trouble. They tramped back to the office, leading their horses from the tie-rails.

Clint figured he had worked as fast as any human could. He got to saddle, swore the mounted possemen in with a rapid gabble of words. They were deputies now for the purpose of the ride!

He heard Hoot was sleeping, having been given a draught by Doc Hawton, so he did not bother the old-timer.

The posse rode out of Laredo without any yippees or Colt firing, which was often the case with the wilder and younger men. Even the rannigans with the whisky were quiet. Soon the town, with its patches of yellow light, was left behind and the horses jogged quickly out to the Circle Four spread.

Clint rode close to Jesse Teed, the rancher. Clint had not seen the cool-headed man since the time Rolf Lester had tried to stamp on his gun-hand and Jesse Teed had intervened. Clint gave the rancher the facts so that he could form a balanced opinion.

'I want them *hombres* brought in fer trial, Jesse,' he said. 'I want 'em to start spillin' the beans about each other. Hoot an' me got evidence stacked against Fogel. I've got two o' his guns. Guess he didn't waste much time buyin' new smokepoles. The main jasper

I want is their boss. I figure he is Dave Lansing, but provin' it ain't so easy.'

He told Jesse a lot more on the ride. Soon the mesquite covered valley which housed the Circle Four ranch buildings came in sight. The riders jogged on, dust swirling up behind them to mark their passage.

The posse did not ride straight up. As the riders approached the ranch, nestling amid the wind breaking cottonwoods, they dismounted and walked the animals slowly forward. Hoof beats could travel far in the night.

Three possemen moved round the ranch, while Clint, Jesse and another rancher walked with a measured tread into the ranchyard and then up to the porch.

Clint put his hand on the door, found it was locked. The windows were shuttered. He hammered sharply.

'Open up – the Law!' he grated.

# 9

# DEAD CITY

There was an appreciable pause and then the door opened slowly. Framed in the dim light glowing from the room, was Mary Lester. Her eyes were wide with fear; her lips parted in a swift intake of breath.

'Howdy, Mary,' said Clint sombrely. 'We've come to take Rolf an' Fogel.'

'They ain't here!'

He did not reply. His face was stern, set. Then:

'Reckon we'll come in, Mary.' His voice was low.

He stepped forward, and her intake of breath became almost a sob. At the same time a man stepped from behind the door, gun in hand and rammed it into Mary's back.

'Don't move, Randall – don't do anythin'!'

Rolf Lester's face was contorted with rage and bestiality. He stood beside his own sister and held the gun in her back. His eyes glinted pure hell and hate at Clint.

'Don't yuh make a move fer thet hogleg o' yourn!'

he rasped in an unrecognisable voice. 'Yuh don't want Mary to git harmed!'

Cold anger welled up in Clint's heart. He could understand reckless living, but this was hell-bent, in-bitten badness.

'Yuh mad, Rolf!' he snapped. 'Yuh wouldn't kill yuhr own sister!'

'Don't make me try!' hissed the other.

'Put thet gun away an' come quietly. I got a posse round the ranch.'

'Yuh ain't foolin' me, Randall. Yuh figger to git us a raw-hide necktie. Jest don't move any closer! Yuh kin start by moving backwards. Bert an' me are comin' out!'

'Yuh won't git away with it.'

Rolf's voice began to drip cold, measured words.

'Git it straight, Randall. Nuthin' ain't gonna stop me a-gittin' outa here! Nuthin'! Yuh don't want Mary hurt. By A'mighty Gawd, I'll use this gun on her if yuh don't drop back!'

The hell-bent young rannigan's words literally dripped brutality. There was no doubt he meant everything he said. Clint swallowed to ease the tightness in his throat. He looked at Mary, saw the fear in her eyes. She could hardly speak, but she stammered:

'Drop back, Clint . . . he's dangerous . . . he'll shoot . . . once he beat me . . . I never told yuh thet . . .'

Clint stepped back, his guns still firm in the palms of his hands. Jesse Teed obeyed Clint's order to stand clear and with the other rancher they stood to one side.

Rolf eased out slowly, with one hand gripping Mary's shoulder. His hand bit into her shirt. She was still dressed for riding. Rolf's gun kept ground into her side. Behind him appeared Fogel. His Colts were out, and his eyes were alight with dangerous glints.

Rolf eased out slowly, with one hand gripping Mary's.

'Yuh kin back down them steps!' he hissed. 'I ain't havin' yuh movin' to the side. Down – and remember, Randall, so help me, I ain't foolin'!'

There was no doubting the buckeroo's savage intention. Clint was thinking furiously. They could outwit Rolf and Fogel by a few swift leaps and flying lead. But Mary would get hurt.

He just did not want to chance that.

Reluctantly, Clint and the other two possemen backed down the steps to the ranch-yard. The other three possemen were out in the darkness, and two of them were on the other side of the ranch house and might not know what was going on.

Slowly and with harsh breathing sounds, Rolf came down the steps, tight behind the girl. Fogel moved so close to Rolf, they were as one.

At the bottom of the steps, Rolf began to move sideways like a crab. There was a certain mastery about his crouching movements.

Jesse Teed burst out.

'Goldarn it, we ain't goin' to let 'em git away!'

He was about to step to one side when Rolf's voice lashed the night air.

'Start shootin' an' Mary's shore to git it! Tell them helliers to start thinkin', Randall!'

Although the night was cooling off, sweat suddenly feelt clammy on Clint's brow.

'Don't do anythin', fellers!' he said thinly. 'Yuh're

dealing with a polecat! He ain't fitten to be alive!'

Rolf was edging to the barn. For every yard he took, accompanied by the helplessly twisting girl and Fogel, the three possemen moved a yard. But they kept in front of the vicious desperate men.

As they went on, Clint suddenly saw the tethered horses near the barn. Three horses stood quietly in the shadow. He detected saddles on them, and one, he felt sure, was packed up with saddle bags. It suddenly struck him – Rolf and Fogel had visited the Circle Four to take away some valuables. Maybe there was gold or stolen money in the bags!

The stalemate had not changed when Rolf got to the horses and with a quick, lithe movement hoisted Mary to one and got up behind her. With a quick leap, Fogel was hitting his leather, too.

Rolf's voice jarred from his throat. He was a bull-tough young rannigan, but even his nerve had been tested by the rain. His voice was hoarse.

'Git back, Randall! We're a-goin'! Start shootin' an' Mary might be the one yuh hit!'

At that moment he fed spurs to the horse's flanks and with a fast spring the animal leaped into stride.

Fogel rode stirrup to stirrup with Rolf. They were in such a hurry they could not take the third horse on a lead rope, and the cayuse was left behind.

While Clint, Jesse Teed and the other rancher justifiably hesitated, Rolf fed steel to his horse and the mount sprang over the ranch yard rails. It was a good leap with double-load. Fogel followed suit.

Stung to anger, Jesse Teed threw hot lead at Fogel as his horse sailed over the fence. Clint heard the man's exclamation of pain and knew he had been hit. But he stuck on his horse and rode after Rolf.

The horsemen began to run forward.

'Tarnation!' howled Jesse Teed. 'We bin done nice!'

Another man swore disgustedly.

Then as they made for their bunched horses outside the ranch yard, they heard the sound of a ratapan of shots. It was followed by the shrill whinnies of spooked horses and then the drum of hoofs as frightened animals raced madly away.

Rolf was smart. He had stampeded the posse's horses!

'Goldarn it!' roared a man. 'Thet cayuse o' mine'll run fer miles if it gits spooked!'

High-heeled boots pounded earth as the men ran out for the animals, but the horses had gone, racing madly away, spooked by suddenly roaring guns.

The night had swallowed Rolf and Fogel, too.

Clint turned and raced back. His vest flapped out with the speed of his movement. He ran back to the barn.

He found the horse with the saddle-bags jogging in a circle, bewildered by the sudden noise. Grabbing the bridle, he calmed it, got to the saddle and rode out of the ranch yard, turning through the gates so sharply the horse was nearly on its haunches.

Clint rode through the running possemen and he bawled out to them

'I'm a-goin' after them galoots! Yuh kin round up yore hosses! I ain't got no time for it!'

'Plug thet dogblastit *hombre* the next time yuh set lamps on him!' Jesse Teed shouted back.

'I'll do thet pretty soon!' vowed Clint.

He did not suppose Jesse Teed heard the last words, but for his own part he meant them, grimly.

There was nothing but implacable anger in his heart against Rolf Lester. The rannigan would stop at nothing. He had risked Mary's life to save his own neck.

Clint rowelled the horse on, not sparing the cayuse, but the animal was laden with the pack bags. He stared ahead through the wan moonlight and wondered which direction the fugitives had taken. He had an idea of the general direction because of the layout of the land and the fact that they would not turn for Laredo. He fed more steel to the snorting animal, and as the ground began to rise, he suddenly saw the shapes of rider and horse outlined against the blue-black sky as they topped the distant ridge.

Then, the next second, they were plunging down the other side, out of sight.

Clint pounded the animal up to the ridge, stared over the darkish land ahead. He could not see the riders. He reined the horse, jumped down and placed his ear to the ground.

It was an old Indian trick. It needed practice and perception to discover from the sound he heard which direction the pounding horses were taking, but he got a good idea of the position of the fleeing riders. He leaped to the leather again and urged the horse on.

He figured if he was hampered by the saddle bags, Rolf Lester would be hampered by the presence of Mary.

The ground under foot was grass-land, with

clumps of thorn bushes. This was the Circle Four's poor quality land, and there would be longhorns somewhere around. The horse swerved more than once to avoid a thorn bush, and Clint had to ride with his usual mastery.

Grimly, he figured that Fogel might be having a bad time of it. Jesse Teed's bullet had hit him. There was no way of telling how bad he was wounded, but the man had undoubtedly stuck to the leather.

Clint did not think that his own head had been creased just that day, and that he was still wearing a bandage. The swift events just pounded the numbness from his head.

He patted the saddle-bags as the horse went on at a full lope. He felt the distinct outline of gold-dust bags. There was also the rustling feel of currency. Too bad Rolf had to make his getaway without his spoils!

He urged the cayuse over the rolling ground and more than once he saw the distant shape of a rider outlined against the bluish-dark sky as they topped a ridge. The sight was merely momentary, and they had a good head start.

For the next hour he trailed them, sometimes getting down from the horse and listening for hoof beats. At other times he had to scan the ground, his face inches from the surface in the darkish night. But he never lost the trail. The grass was left behind and the familiar arid conditions came into view. Gaunt Joshua trees loomed suddenly out of the darkness. His horse was tiring, but he figured that Rolf Lester's mount must he pretty much the same.

There was no sound of oncoming riders from

behind him. The posse was badly left behind. Maybe some had still not got their horses!

All at once, like a savage reminder that this was a grim trail of death, he saw a pale face staring at him from ahead. He saw the shape of a person – and he scooped at his guns.

He never fired them.

The person ahead was Mary Lester. She had heard him approach and was waving her arms.

'Clint! Oh, Clint! Thank heavens! They set me down here – alone!'

'The mangey coyote!' he swore. 'I might ha' passed yuh in the dark. Yuh might ha' got lost!'

'I know where they are going!' she choked.

'Whar, Mary?'

'They're headin' for the City of the Moon!' she gasped.

He dismounted and held her in his arms.

'Thet's the old Injun city, carved out o' living rock in the hills! Why'n heck are they goin' there?'

'I don't know. But I heard Fogel mention the City of the Moon. Fogel is hit bad. He can't ride for ever. He's got a bullet in his shoulder an' it's bleedin' bad.'

He held her tight, one arm round her shoulder while he stared into the silent, eerie land around them. There was a sphinx-like feeling about the brooding terrain as it lay under the wan moon.

'They won't reach the City o' the Moon till nigh on sunup,' he muttered. 'I don't git it. There ain't nuthin' there but rocks and rattlers. There was a spring, but maybe it's dried up.'

'Well, I heard Fogel say somethin' about "when we git to the City o' the Moon" and Rolf sort of nodded.'

Clint made up his mind.

'All right, Mary, we've got to ride back. Thet land ahead is too tough fer you.'

'But I want to go along with you!'

'Yuh can't,' he said quietly. 'It ain't the place for you. An' this hoss can't take two an' these saddle bags an' still have some steam for an emergency. Nope; we got to ride back. Maybe, we'll meet up with the posse. Them fellers will shore be on the prod!'

Mary climbed to the horse with Clint's help, and a few minutes later the animal was cantering back over its own trail to the Circle Four. Clint was guided by his own instinct and knowledge of the shadowy terrain around him.

In this way, they rode back for a few miles. Mary's nearness was strangely exhilarating to Clint Randall. He was a hardish young man, and not a *hombre* for gallivanting with women. There was only one woman for him, and that was Mary. He wanted her for his wife. Included in his stern, rigid code was the belief that a good wife was the best thing a man could possess in this tough country of the west. And in addition to this belief was the feeling of love he had for this girl.

Mary was forgetting the malicious things Rolf had told her about Clint. She knew, as she sat close to him, that Clint was fine – and that that be loved her. It was a marvellous feeling, and everything was suddenly clear and uncomplicated. Rolf would go on and on. There was nothing more she could do.

She had done all she could to help her brother. She would still be willing to help him – but Rolf was past her help now, she knew.

A few miles from the Circle Four ranch buildings, they rode into two members of the posse who were searching for sign. When Clint related the events, they rode back a bit further and after a few penetrating shouts rang over the silent land, and the other possemen rode up.

Mary was taken back to the ranch, and the saddle-bags were stowed away in a safe place for future evidence.

Clint was careful about the saddle-bags. He realized that the contents would prove the case against Rolf and Fogel. But what he wanted was proof against Dave Lansing.

He found his own horse nosing for grass against the rails of a corral near the ranch house. There was his rifle, still in the saddle boot. He needed that.

Minutes later the posse rode out plumb bent for the City of the Moon. They were muttering curses to themselves. Each man figured he had been fooled, and he did not like it.

They rode fast in an effort to make up for lost time. Clint rode up beside Jesse Teed, and they headed out over the Circle Four land.

After an hour of hard riding the land gradually merged into arid desert conditions again. It was scrub-land, with clumps of mesquite grass between the patches of cholla. The leery Texas longhorns might find food out here, but they would have to walk the beef off themselves to get it!

The posse rode in a bunch, now at a fast jog. As another hour passed, the land flattened out into desert pure and simple. The patches of cholla cactus became more and more infrequent. The horses' hoofs dug into hard gypsum sand, corrugated by sun into a million ridges. The posse headed straight into the desert. Clint knew the desert was about eight to nine miles in extent and the hills that housed the City of the Moon rose abruptly out of the desolate expanse.

The horses slowed to a dogged walk, and the men were silent. The moon was riding high and the night was eerie. The silence was absolute. There was no living thing for miles, except, perhaps, for some rattlers in the occasional patch of shale and rock. The City of the Moon was an ancient site of a long forgotten tribe of Indians. The caves and homes, temples and store chambers, were cut out of the cliff face and still endured to this day, although wind and rain had scoured the outside carvings. It was a spooky sort of place, Clint knew; and the present day Indians avoided the site. It was 'bad medicine'.

They rode on and on, riding into the steep slopes and skirting the smooth round pits of sand. Clint had set a course by the stars. The horses plodded methodically over the monotonously undulating sand.

As the hills came into view, the dawn came with a pale glow of watery light superseding the moon. Then soon the moon disappeared from view. It was early sunup.

Tired riders suddenly saw horses' hoof-marks stretching ahead. Two horses had ridden that way.

It was corroboration, and they rode on. The horses were tired, but Rolf's and Fogel's cayuses would be just as weary.

One thing puzzled Clint Randall. Why should Rolf

and Fogel head out this way? They were still in Texas. They could have used the horses to get away into Mexico, and would have been beyond Clint Randall or Hoot Sampson's authority.

There was some reason and no doubt it would soon become clear. The posse rode slowly up to the hills. They rose like huge heaps of rock and shale as if they had been thrown carelessly on to the desert.

There was no vegetation - nothing but the reddish-yellow sand and rock. The place brooded.

They rode in closer and could see the caves studding the cliff face. Curious openings and weathered carvings were the entrances to temples cut into the rock. Narrow, crumbling tracks led to these openings. Some of them were high in the cliff face.

'Don't see no hosses!' announced Jesse Teed.

In the shelter of a rocky outcrop, the posse dismounted and ground hitched the animals. Rifles were taken from saddle boots, and the men gathered in a knot for further discussion. It was brief.

'If those *hombres* are thar, we've got to git 'em out,' said Clint. 'So spread out an' move up. They'll give themselves away, iffen they are still there.'

# 10

# VULTURE TRAIL

When Mary was left alone at the Circle Four, she sat down and naturally gave herself over to thought.

She pictured the grim posse riding out to the ancient City of the Moon – as the Indians called it – and she thought of Rolf. They were either hiding there, for some reason or other, or they were making a visit and would ride on. But to where? Would Rolf ever return to the ranch?

She wished she could stop thinking about him – thinking of him as a boy growing up on this very ranch. And there had been Tad, just as wild and reckless as Rolf. Something in their blood had impelled them on to a lawless life.

The ranch was being neglected. Right now there was only Tom Week in the bunkhouse Although the spread was not a rich one, it could be improved if work was done.

But now there was no one to do it.

Restlessly, she rose and picked up some needlework. A knock sounded on the door.

She went to the door, but did not open it. She called out 'Who is there?'

'Let me in, Mary. It's Dave Lansing. Rolf an' Fogel there?'

She did not open the door. She was glad it was bolted from the inside. The windows were shuttered, too. She moved determinedly across the room and picked up a shotgun. Swiftly, she loaded it with two cartridges.

She returned to the door. 'They are not here,' she said.

'How come? We arranged to meet up hyar. I'm a bit late, as a matter o' fact.'

'The posse are after them!' she hissed.

'Is thet so? Where they headin'? Maybe I kin do something to help them jiggers.'

'You figure yore skin is safe, don't yuh?' snapped Mary.

She heard him laugh.

'Maybe. Where the rannigans gone, Mary? I kin help 'em, yuh know.'

She saw no reason why she should not tell him.

'They're headin' for the City of the Moon. I jest don't know why.'

She heard his sudden exclamation, and then his curse.

'The double-crossin' rats! Wal, thet settles it. Those hellions won't git away from the posse. But I'm a-goin' while thet doggone deputy is out there. Adios, Mary, I'm pullin' up stakes and lighting out for Mexico. Plenty o' dinero down by the Rio Grande for a feller like me. I've sold the Bonanza, made the deal today. Well, Rolf is a blamed fool. Him and

Fogel might git thet currency we hid up there, but they won't git out o' thet desert. There ain't any water this time' o' the year in thet Injun town.'

His laugh brought a red cloud of anger across her eyes. She heard him stamp over the porch. He would get away while Rolf paid the penalty!

With consuming anger in her heart, she slipped the bolts back noiselessly.

Opening the door, she saw his dark figure moving down the porch steps.

'Dave Lansing!' she called.

He turned, saw the levelled shotgun and whipped at a Derringer he kept in a shoulder holster inside his coat.

The shotgun roared death.

Mary staggered backwards with the kick of the stock. She felt suddenly sick and the anger oozed out of her, leaving her horrified.

She dared not look at the huddled body beyond the porch steps.

She knew Lansing was dead.

As Tom Week came to the bunkhouse door, she ran into the house and bolted the door again. She sank to a seat and pressed her fingers to her temples.

Clint Randall walked slowly up the incline, rifle in hand, his keen eyes searching the holes in the cliff face. He was watching for sudden movement of any black figure against the yellow cliffs. He was watching for horses; too. Somewhere in the rabbit-warren of crumbling caves and hollowed-out homes, Rolf and Fogel might be lurking.

He was still unsure about their motives. What in

the heck had brought the two *hombres* across the desert to this ancient site?

The dawn was becoming lighter now. There was a cool breeze moving softly across the land, but when he put his hand to the desert the white gypsum was still warm with yesterday's sun.

The remainder of the posse were moving slowly forward from different directions. They were near to the crumbling shale incline that led to one ledge and the mouths of the caves.

'I'll give 'em a shout,' Clint called to Jesse Teed.

Clint raised his voice.

'Hello, there!'

The echoes came back at him suddenly with a ghostly 'hello, there'. Then there was silence.

Clint tried again.

'We're a-comin' for yuh, Lester! Come on out. Yuh, too, Fogel!'

But only silence reigned after the echoes died away.

'Maybe they ain't there,' said Jesse Teed. 'Maybe they've ridden on.'

Then from somewhere in the caves a shot rang out. A second later another Colt barked inside the ancient holes. The died echoes away, and the posse-men looked at each other for no bullet had come their way.

'Them fellers are a-fightin'!' said Jesse Teed.

'Could be,' agreed Clint grimly.

Rolf and Fogel had found the hidden currency. The greater portion of the loot was Dave Lansing's, and the bills were too hot to circulate. It had been

Lansing's idea to cache them out in this old Indian site, for the simple reason that no one ever came to the place. Later, when it was possible to spend the money or change it into other notes in order to bank it, he had intended to split the loot.

They lifted the stones from the hidden cavity and withdrew the bundles of money. Fogel's eyes were glinting with pain and greed. The red patch on his shoulder was sapping his strength. Rolf, eyeing him grimly, knew it.

'There's a cave runs right back through the hill from hyar,' grunted Rolf. 'Kinda tunnel. But yuh can't git a hoss through. Some places the tunnel is only three feet high.'

They had the money divided into two heaps. Rolf began to stuff his share into his shirt, cramming it inside, next to his skin.

'What'll we do on the other side without a hoss?' snapped Fogel.

'Walk!' Rolf grinned at him. 'Yuh can't git back to the hosses, feller. It's daylight. An' listen!'

They heard the sound of a man's voice hailing them.

'*We're a-comin' for yuh Lester! Come on out. Yuh, too Fogel!*'

'That's 'em,' said Rolf, and he cursed evilly. 'There ain't no goin' back fer the hosses.'

'I can't walk far – yuh know thet!' snarled Fogel. 'Ain't it desert on the other side?'

'Yep. About five miles on there's an Indian encampment. They've got cayuses. We'll make it afore them *hombres* figger we gone.'

'Five miles o' desert!' snarled Fogel. 'I don't like!

This blasted bit o' lead in my shoulder is givin' me hell!'

Rolf smiled.

'Git yore dinero stowed away. Yuh kin try. Too bad if yuh don't make it.'

Fogel's eyes narrowed, and then dull rage tinged his cheeks.

He made to pick up some of the bills, but his hand whipped to his gun instead.

He scooped it out and it blasted.

But Rolf had seen the play. His gun spoke at the same time.

Rolf felt a slug bite into him. The impact made him stagger back and he tripped.

When he looked up, smiling, Fogel had died. There was a jagged hole in his head and blood bubbled sickeningly.

Rolf took out the thick wad of notes from inside his shirt and looked at them. Somewhere in them a slug was embedded. The wad had stopped Fogel's bullet.

'Kinda spoilt them bills!' chuckled Rolf, and he threw the stolen currency to one side.

He knew he had been lucky, but the thought did not sober him. Instead he felt triumphant, taking it as a symbol of his ever-lasting luck.

He would get through to the Indian camp. The Indians had ponies. He'd be all right.

Fogel had guessed he had only wanted the jigger to carry the rest of the money until he dropped from heat and exhaustion. Fogel had gone for his gun because he knew he was finished and he wanted to take the other with him.

Rolf grinned. He was not going the way of Fogel. He could cross the desert on the other side of the hill.

He began to pack the money all around him. The bills were bulky, but he did not intend to leave any, except the wad with the embedded slug.

Finally he was ready. He had only Colts with him. His rifle was in the saddle boot and the horse was ground hitched near the entrance to the cave. He figured he could do without the rifle.

Finally he was ready to leave. He began to walk forward. Light filtered through into the cave at this point from a few crevices in the roof. But after a few yards the visibility became dim. He was sure of the way, and he congratulated himself upon the fact that he had actually made the trip once before.

Clint had shrewdly estimated the spot from where the sound of the shots had emerged. He was the first to run forward, his eyes fixed on the small arch at the end of a broad ledge running across the cliff face. The remainder of the posse came with him, but he was first up to the cave mouth.

He walked more carefully as he approached the mouth. He sidled along the face of the rock, peered into the first few yards of the silent place, wondering if a gun would roar at him. He turned into the jagged mouth, and saw the two horses ground hitched in the cover of a bluff. Getting behind the horses, he saw that the wanted men had left their rifles in saddle boots. He moved into the cave, saw that the light was not bad now that his eyes were accustomed to it.

He passed a white skeleton on the way, and knew some wanderer had lain down to die some time in

the past. The walls of the cave bore evidence of carvings and ornamental stonework. He merely flicked a
glance at them. A rustle prompted him to raise the
rifle suddenly. Looking up to the roof he saw three
black vultures perched in a roosting place. Three
black vultures! The birds of ill-omen!

He moved on determinedly. Behind him Jesse
Teed and the other men strode slowly forward.

They came to the chamber where Bert Fogel lay.

'Shore figgered they was fightin',' said Jesse Teed.

'And this is what they were fightin' about,' declared
Clint, and he held up the wad of currency and looked
curiously at the embedded slug.

'Shore got hell's own luck!' commented Jesse
Teed.

Clint threw it away and strode down the cave. He
had a sudden hunch that Rolf Lester had means of
escape. He had killed Fogel and left the horses. The
rannigan must have some plan. Clint went ahead
with all speed. The light dimmed, but he ran on,
running from boulder to boulder. The floor was
strewn with fallen rock. Evidently the cave had a
tendency to crumble. He sped on, one hand
outstretched in the dim light, the other gripping the
rifle.

The tunnel was narrowing and the roof was low.
After a few more yards, Clint had to move at a
crouch.

His eyes ached with the strain of peering through
the dimness. Hearing the clatter of boots on rock just
ahead, he edged round a huge fallen rock that
almost blocked the path and then halted.

Rolf had heard his movement.

A gun spat red flame from the darkness.

Clint's rifle roared in instant challenge before the Colt flame had died away.

Clint felt the angry rush of wind as a slug tore past his head. Then, with horrible suddenness, came the ominous rumble of crashing rock. He heard a shrill, wild yell and then more rumbles. He knew, in that split second, that his shot had not killed Rolf Lester.

But as he staggered back, round the obtruding rock, his mouth full of dust and his ears filled with the thunder of falling rock, he knew that Rolf was dead.

The two shots had brought down the crumbling cave roof. Clint staggered back as the dust surged after him. He went until he ran into the possemen.

'He's dead,' he said, 'an' buried!'


They rode back across the desert almost immediately, taking as evidence the wad of currency with the embedded slug.

Clint began to smile thinly, tiredly. Once more he was riding in to Laredo, tired and stooped in the saddle. Once more he was leaving a dead Lester back in the waste-land. But he was sure this time Mary would understand. This time she would listen to him, agree with him. It was his job to help her forget her hellbent brothers.

He looked at the rising sun, saw in it the promise of another day. That was a good idea. There was always another day for those with faith. And he had faith in his future life with Mary.

He began to grin.

'Say, Jesse, I figger we're headin' for a weddin'!'
'Jest let me guess the rest!' said Jesse, grinning
broadly.